D0089756

ALSO BY

ANDREA CAMILLERI

The Revolution of the Moon
The Sacco Gang

THE SECT OF ANGELS

Andrea Camilleri

THE SECT OF ANGELS

Translated by Stephen Sartarelli

Europa Editions
214 West 29th Street
New York, N.Y. 10001
www.europaeditions.com
info@europaeditions.com

This book is a work of fiction. Any references to historical events, real people, or real locales are used fictitiously.

First Publication 2019 by Europa Editions

Translation by Stephen Sartarelli
Original title: *La setta degli angeli*

Library of Congress Cataloging in Publication Data is available
ISBN 978-1-60945-513-2

Camilleri, Andrea
The Sect of Angels

Book design by Emanuele Ragnisco
www.mekkanografici.com

Cover image: Fauk74 / Alamy Stock Photo

Prepress by Grafica Punto Print – Rome

Printed in the USA

CONTENTS

THE SECT OF ANGELS

Chapter I
The Matter of the Marbles

Gentlemen! Members of the club! A moment of your attention, please!" said don Liborio Spartà, president of the Honor and Family Social Club. "I will now open the urn and begin counting the marbles."

The buzz of voices in the drawing room gradually hushed to a relative silence. Relative, that is, because don Anselmo Buttafava had, as usual, fallen asleep in the damask armchair he'd sat in for the past thirty years and more, and was snoring so loud that the windowpanes giving onto the balcony in front of him were rattling lightly. Although the club had changed all the furniture some ten years earlier, they could do nothing about that armchair: they'd had to leave it in its place, for the exclusive use and enjoyment of don Anselmo.

"What's that burning smell?" Commendatore Paladino asked aloud just as the president opened the urn.

"So you smell it, too?" retired Colonel Petrosillo asked the commendatore in turn.

"I do too!" said Professor Malatesta.

"It's true!" said many of those present. "There's something burning!"

As everyone was wrinkling his nose and looking around left and right, trying to determine where the burning smell was coming from, don Serafino Labianca cried out:

"There's smoke coming from don Anselmo!"

They all turned to look at don Anselmo, who kept on snoring, head hanging down to his chest. And indeed they saw an ever so fine column of smoke rising up from the armchair towards the ceiling, which had been frescoed by Angelino Vasalicò, a carriage painter and local celebrity, and dubbed "better than the Sistine Chapel!" by the mayor, Nicolò Calandro.

The first to pinpoint the source of the smoke was don Stapino Vassallo, perhaps because he was the youngest member present and still had good eyesight, being only forty-two years of age, whereas the average age of the others was around sixty.

"The cigar!"

He ran up to the damask armchair.

Don Anselmo's cigar had in fact slipped from his sleeping hand and fallen onto his trousers, in the very spot where the male pudenda are usually tucked away. The ember had already burnt through the dense English fabric of his trousers and was now attacking the thick wool of his underpants.

As don Stapino was dashing over to the president's table to grab the pitcher of water on it, Colonel Petrosillo, a man of action, quickly crouched down between don Anselmo's legs and with his left hand snatched up the cigar, throwing it to the floor, while with his right hand he began vigorously patting the areas in danger of catching fire.

Awakened by a sudden blow to his cojones, don Anselmo Buttafava, seeing the colonel between his legs, got the wrong idea. For some time now, nasty rumors had been circulating about town concerning the excessive fondness that Amasio Petrosillo, who had never married, seemed to have for a certain Ciccino, the twenty-year-old son of the colonel's farm overseer. Instinctively, therefore, don Anselmo pushed the colonel's face away brusquely, causing him to fall backwards, then got up and ran towards the president's table yelling like a madman.

"I've always known that Petrosillo is a big pervert! Out of this club, now!"

President Spartà tried to clear things up.

"Don Anselmo, there's been a mistake! The colonel, you see . . . "

But don Anselmo, who by habit lit up like a match at the slightest provocation, was by this point extremely worked up and wouldn't listen to reason.

"Either he goes or I go!"

"But, don Anselmo, if you would just listen to me for a second . . . "

"Then I'll go myself!"

And with a violent sweep of the arm he swatted the urn, which fell to the floor and, having already been opened, sent all the marbles rolling across the room, as don Anselmo ran into the privy, cursing like a Turk, and locked the door.

Between one thing and another—with the colonel shouting and bleeding from the nose after don Anselmo's shove, the president wanting to resign immediately, and the secretary scrambling about trying to pick the marbles up off the floor—a squabble arose between those who thought don Anselmo was in the right and those who thought he was in the wrong. It took a good half an hour to settle things down again.

"We must all recast our votes. The gentlemen members must vote whether or not to admit Attorney Matteo Teresi to the club. A black marble means no, a white marble means yes. There are twenty-nine members present, since Baron Lo Mascolo sent word that he couldn't take part, and Doctor Bellanca did the same, and don Anselmo Buttafava is now—"

"—is now present. And so there are thirty members voting," said don Anselmo, appearing in a secondary doorway in the salon.

Colonel Petrosillo, still holding a wet handkerchief over his nose, stood up and said:

"I man the peak."

Everyone fell silent in bewilderment, wondering what

bizarre military fantasy the colonel might have of sending a garrison to some unnamed mountaintop. The only person to grasp the situation was, as usual, don Stapino Vassallo.

"Colonel, please be so kind as to lower your handkerchief and repeat your statement."

The colonel complied.

"I demand to speak."

"Please go ahead," said the president.

"I hereby publicly declare that don Anselmo should consider himself slapped by me, and therefore challenged to a duel. So, for my seconds I should like to name—"

"Can't we talk about this later?" asked the president.

"All right," said the colonel.

They cast their votes.

When the urn was reopened, out came twenty-nine black marbles, signifying twenty-nine "no" votes, and one white marble, signifying one "yes." Since the vote had not been unanimous, the matter had to be raised again for discussion and then voted on a second time, as every decision concerning a potential new member had to be unanimous.

Don Liborio Spartà decided to intervene.

"Gentlemen. Since today is Sunday, the midday Mass will be starting in half an hour. And we must all go. I therefore propose a waiver of the rule concerning abbreviations of procedure. Are you all in agreement?"

"Yes, yes," said many voices.

"As we know, gentlemen, every new candidate for membership must, according to the rules, be presented by two associates of the club with more than five years' membership. In the present case, those sponsoring the candidacy of Attorney Matteo Teresi were Baron Lo Mascolo, absent, and Marquis don Filadelfo Cammarata, here present. Clearly, the white marble could only have been put in the urn by my lord Marquis Cammarata, to whom I politely request—"

"Clearly, my arse!" said the angry marquis.

Don Filadelfo Cammarata was about fifty, skinny as a rail, married and the father of eight daughters, all fine churchgoing young ladies, and he was always upset about something, always arguing with someone and quick to resort to vulgar language. Even when alone, he could often be seen gesticulating animatedly—arguing with himself.

"My good marquis, simple logic leads me to—"

"Simple logic leads you up your own anus," the marquis retorted, standing up. "And I'm saying that, both the first and the second time, the vote I cast was a black marble!"

Everyone looked bewildered.

"What?" they said. "But it was you who presented him for membership!"

"And then I changed my mind, all right? Is a man not free to change his mind?"

"*I* can tell you why you changed your mind!" don Serafino Labianca said with an insinuating smile from the far end of the room.

It was well known that the two men were not fond of each other. Don Serafino was a liberal and a Freemason, the marquis was a Papist and man of the Church, and they were also at odds over a lawsuit more than twenty years old concerning the disputed ownership of a cherry tree.

All at once the marquis's face, already red, turned green. Traffic lights did not exist at the time, otherwise the similarity would have been striking.

"And just what are you, Serafino by name but a horned devil in fact, trying to insinuate?"

"Please, gentlemen, for pity's sake!" the president beseeched them.

Don Serafino took no offense.

"I'm not insinuating anything. You sued Father Raccuglia, claiming he'd taken possession of a piece of your land exactly the same way you've taken people's cherry trees away, and so you turned to the lawyer Teresi, who eats priests for dinner, roasted, fried, or topped with tomato sauce . . . Is that true or not?"

"Yes, it's true! So what? What the hell is your point? It doesn't mean that when somebody turns to a lawyer he has to embrace his political ideas as well!"

"Let me finish. The lawyer agreed to sue on your behalf, but he also asked you to support his candidacy for membership in the club. Which you did."

"I certainly couldn't refuse a common courtesy such—"

"Courtesy, my eye! The lawyer told you that if you supported his candidacy he would handle your case free of charge. And you, despite your wealth, are as stingy as a dried-up riverbed, you couldn't believe your ears!"

"So then why did I vote against him, can you tell me that?"

"Of course I can. The lawsuit had barely begun when Father Raccuglia let himself be persuaded, by someone acting on your behalf, that he should admit he was in the wrong. And so, just like that, no more lawsuit. So you, who had turned to Attorney Teresi—the only man in town with the cheek to sue a priest—immediately turned your back on him. Therefore, as you can see, I didn't insinuate anything."

"No, you are insinuating that I had someone act on my behalf! So, why don't we start with you naming his name?"

"Oh, no you don't! No names! That's enough of that! Let's end this! It's getting late!" shouted a number of voices.

It was of utmost importance that the person's name not be revealed. The arguments were starting to take a dangerous turn. And the name that mustn't be mentioned was that of *'u zù* Carmineddru, the town's Mafia chieftain, a man of honor and consequence.

"In that case, gentlemen, after the marquis's declaration, I have no choice but to address my words to the unknown member who . . . "

"So how do you explain that two noblemen, Baron Lo Mascolo and Marquis Cammarata, turned to a lawyer like Teresi, who's a known instigator?" asked don Serafino with his usual smile, taking advantage of the momentary silence to slip in a question that everyone, truth be told, had been asking themselves.

"I will break your bones, God help me!" exclaimed the marquis, jumping up from his chair and hurling himself at his adversary.

He never reached him, however, as three men managed to restrain him. Frothing at the mouth like an enraged bull, the marquis stormed out of the meeting.

"Gentlemen, gentlemen, please! Let's get this over with quick. The bell has already rung for the Mass. I therefore address myself to the unknown—"

"And when are we going to talk about the duel?" asked Colonel Petrosillo, whose nosebleed wouldn't stop, enraging him further with every passing minute.

"Later, later," they all said in a sort of chorus.

"Then I beg the unknown member who voted for admission please to explain to the rest of us—" the president began.

"There's no damn need to beg," said don Anselmo Buttafava. "I was the one who voted yes."

"Why?" asked the president. "I believe you said several times in the past you never wanted to see Teresi in here, not even dead."

"And in fact in the first round of voting I voted no."

"So why did you change your mind?"

"Because if there's a pervert like Colonel Petrosillo in this club I don't see why we can't admit a Bakuninist like the lawyer Teresi."

"Good point," commented don Serafino, who that Sunday morning seemed determined to get on the nerves of all of creation.

Colonel Petrosillo shot to his feet, as pale as a corpse.

"Consider yourself slapped likewise!" he said to don Serafino.

"I don't consider myself anything at all. Come over here and slap me in person, if you're man enough. And since your bum has already been thrashed, I'll get to work on your face, just to finish what don Anselmo started."

The colonel opened his mouth to reply, but at that moment a nervous twitch came over his face. He immediately stiffened, eyes rolling back into his head, and fell backwards. He suffered from occasional epileptic fits. A good fifteen minutes were lost in the efforts to revive him and accompany him to his carriage.

"May I have permission to speak, Mr. President, sir?" asked Giallonardo the notary.

"You may."

"Just now you said that the sponsors of Attorney Teresi's candidacy were Marquis don Filadelfo Cammarata and Baron Lo Mascolo, correct?"

"Correct."

"Then, since don Filadelfo admitted to having twice cast a black marble vote, the fact of having repeated the same gesture would serve to invalidate, essentially, his prior sponsorship—indeed annul it entirely. Therefore, things being so, Attorney Teresi's candidacy can be considered to have been advanced by only one signature, that of Baron Lo Mascolo. Now, according to the rules, only one sponsor is not enough. Ergo, it is as if Attorney Teresi never made any request for admission."

"Well, I'll be damned! Brilliant!" don Stapino Vassallo said in admiration.

"Seems to make perfect sense to me," said the president. "Are the gentlemen members in agreement that . . . ?"

"Yes! Yes!"

The chorus was unanimous.

"Then the session is adjourned," said the president.

There was a mad dash for the door, legs flying, arms pushing, as the members of the club ran to catch the last Mass in their respective churches.

*

A town of seven thousand inhabitants located right in the middle of the great *latifondi* estates, Palizzolo, in the year 1901, could boast of having two marquis, four barons, a one-hundred-and-two-year-old duke who no longer set foot outside his castle, and an anti-Bourbon martyr, attorney Ruggero Colapane, hanged in the public square for having supported the Parthenopean Republic.[1]

But its greatest source of pride was its eight churches, each endowed with a bell tower and bells so powerful that when they rang all together in unison, it felt just like an earthquake inside people's houses.

Seven of these eight churches had been divvied up between the nobility and landowners on the basis of mutual antipathies and sympathies, familial relations acknowledged or denied, longstanding resentments and quarrels dating back to the times of Carlos Quinto, and civil suits hailing from the age of Frederick II of Swabia and carried on even after the Unification of Italy, as well as undying hatreds and changing attachments.

And so, for example, you would never have seen, say, someone like don Stapino Vassallo and someone like don Filadelfo Cammarata attending Mass together at the church of Our Lady of Sorrows, whose parish priest was Patre Don Angelo Marrafà.

[1] A short-lived, French-inspired and French-supported republican revolution that seized the city of Naples, under Bourbon rule, in 1799, only to be put down later that year.

In 1514, an ancestor of don Stapino—more specifically the beautiful young Attanasia—had been married at age sixteen to an ancestor of the Marquis Cammarata, a forty-year-old by the name of Adalgiso. After two years of a marriage ratified but never consummated, owing to a case of *impotentia coeundi* on the husband's part, Attanasia could no longer stand living like a cloistered nun despite being married, so she started looking around. And soon, by dint of looking, she found herself impregnated, apparently by a stable hand. Adalgiso sent his wife back to her parents, calling her a trollop. Attanasia riposted by saying that her husband couldn't perform his husbandly duties, because his thingy was as soft as ricotta cheese. This gave rise to lawsuits, trials, and litigations, the result of which was that the two families not only ceased greeting each other in public but indeed never missed an opportunity to do one another a bad turn.

The eighth church, the Church of the Most Holy Crucifix, with the seventy-year-old Don Mariano Dalli Cardillo as its priest, was attended neither by nobles nor by landowners, and not even by the bourgeoisie. It was the church of the peasants and the poor, of those who lived on bread and air.

*

"Beloved children," said Don Alessio Terranova, priest of the parish of San Giovanni, opening his Gospel sermon. "I find myself obliged today to talk to you about a serious matter. A petty newssheet edited and paid for by a local lawyer whose name I won't mention, since it would sully my tongue, and distributed here and in nearby towns, featured an article in this morning's edition in which, on top of the customary insults hurled at the Holy Mother Church and at those of us who represent her in all our unworthiness, the writer mocks the sacrament of holy matrimony and the virginity of maidens and ridicules modesty, chastity, and feminine virtue . . . And so I exhort you, my beloved children—especially my beloved daughters—not to listen to such iniquities, which are clearly inspired by the devil. Virginity is the noblest gift a young bride can give to her legitimate spouse; it is in every way comparable to a flower, which . . . "

*

Patre Raccuglia, head of the town's Mother Church, its most ancient, also said during his sermon that Palizzolo was facing a grave danger, that of ending up just like Sodom and Gomorrah, if the sacrilegious ideas of a little lawyer who loved to pretend he was the people's advocate, when he was in fact the devil's advocate, continued to spread. This man—if a Godless person who disdained family, religion, and country, and every divinely blessed thing on earth, could really be called a man—this man had written in his newssheet that virginity, that supreme gift of maidens, was merely a commodity for purchase! Something that a man could simply buy for cash with a wedding ring! Blasphemy! Whereas virginity was, in fact . . .

*

That Sunday, at the end of the Mass, Giallonardo the notary stopped to talk with don Liborio Spartà outside the church of San Cono, the patron saint of Palizzolo, whose parish priest was Don Filiberto Cusa.

"There's something I don't understand," said the notary. "Why did Teresi request admission to the club when he must have known he would never be accepted?"

"In my opinion," said don Liborio, "he wants to brag about it."

"With whom?"

"With the clients he defends. The ragamuffins, shirkers,

and subversives who don't have an honorable bone in their bodies . . . He'll probably tell them: 'See? The nobles, the bourgeois, the landowners don't want me in their club. And that proves that I'm one of you!'"

"I just can't imagine what that man's got in his head," the notary said pensively. "He let his father, don Masino, who was a very fine person, die of a broken heart. What? You studied to become a pharmacist and that's not enough for you? Nosirree. He goes and gets that law degree, disowns his family and the class he belongs to, and starts doing what he's doing now. The guy's stirring up the riffraff to the point that one of these days, a revolution's going to break out in Palizzolo!"

"Well, the man is certainly dangerous, as far as that goes," said don Liborio.

"Maybe we should give the matter some thought," said the notary, seeing Don Filiberto, the parish priest, come out of the church and begin to approach them, waving his hands in the air by way of greeting.

"I saw you, you know!" said Don Filiberto. "You came late to Mass! Why's that?"

"We had a trying morning at the club," replied don Liborio.

"Why, what happened?"

"We voted on whether to accept lawyer Teresi's request for admission," said the notary.

"And how did it turn out?" asked the priest, his jocund face turning suddenly serious.

"It was considered invalid."

"And a good thing too! If you'd accepted it I would have denied you the sacraments! And you know what else? This Teresi, when he dies, will even have trouble getting into Hell! The devil won't want him!"

They all laughed.

*

Having just come out of the church of the Heart of Jesus, whose priest was Don Alighiero Scurria, Commendatore Paladino and don Serafino Labianca set out, as they did every Sunday morning, on their way to the Gran Caffè Garibaldi to drink their customary glass of malmsey before going to lunch. While don Serafino was certainly a liberal and a Freemason, deep down he feared that God might exist after all, and so, taking the good with the bad, he made a point never to miss a Sunday Mass.

They sat down at a table and started talking, inevitably, about Matteo Teresi.

"His request for membership was just a ruse to provoke us," said the commendatore.

"That's clear," don Serafino agreed.

"But it would be a mistake to react to his provocations, don't you think?"

"Yes, I completely agree."

"On the other hand, we can hardly put up with this forever."

"Patience does have its limits."

"And I'm afraid that sooner or later this man will do some damage, some very grave damage. Don't you think?"

"Absolutely!"

"Don Serafino, at the club you asked an intelligent question but you never gave us the answer."

"I don't remember. What was it?"

"How is it that two noblemen sponsored Teresi's candidacy?"

Don Serafino smiled.

"But it's precisely because of what you've just finished saying! They're afraid that lawyer will stir up the riffraff to the point where all hell breaks loose. So, just to be safe, they want to keep him close."

The waiter brought the two glasses of malmsey, and the men drank in silence.

"Maybe," don Serafino resumed, "we need to discuss this with some other friends of ours. I'd say it's rather urgent. And then we'll meet back up at my house."

"Sounds to me like a good idea," said the commendatore.

Professor Ubaldo Malatesta, superintendent of the local elementary schools—the only schools in Palizzolo—walked into the sacristy of the church of the Most Holy Virgin as the parish priest, Don Libertino Samonà, was removing his vestments with the help of a little boy.

"Why didn't you come to serve Mass today?" asked Don Libertino.

The professor, a shy man, blushed in shame.

"I'm here to apologize. I was detained at the club, and—"

"What?! So you've come to tell me that your gambling vice kept you away—"

"No, Father, there were no games this morning. We were voting on whether to admit Teresi the lawyer to the club."

Patre Samonà was a good six feet tall and six feet wide. Pointing a finger that looked like a cudgel at Professor Malatesta, he asked in a Last-Judgment tone of voice:

"And how did *you* vote?"

"I . . . I voted 'no.'"

"Well, you should know that had you voted 'yes,' not only would I never again have let you serve Holy Mass, I would have chased you right out of the church with so many kicks in the pants you wouldn't be able to sit down for a week!"

Chapter II
The Passion and Flight of don Anselmo

Don Anselmo, for his part, was unable to attend Mass at the church of Saints Cosma and Damiano, whose parish priest was Don Ernesto Pintacuda, because he'd had to go home to change his singed trousers.

And so, since there was still a while to go before lunchtime, he decided to pay a call on Baron Lo Mascolo, first of all to find out whether he'd recovered from the touch of flu that he said he'd come down with two days before, and secondly to ask him to explain why he'd supported Teresi's request.

Don Anselmo, being a good friend of the baron's even though don Fofò was a good twenty years his junior, knew him inside and out, and, truth be told, didn't believe for a minute this business about him having the flu. It was well known that the baron was the picture of good health and had never spent a day in his life in bed, had never had a toothache, never a bellyache, even though he was capable of eating two roast suckling goats with a few kilos of potatoes all by himself.

And so? What's two plus two? Clearly don Fofò, after first supporting lawyer Teresi's request for membership, came to regret it and changed his mind, just as his friend, Marquis Cammarata, had done, and instead of going to the club and voting with a black marble, he decided to pretend he was sick.

Don Anselmo had just raised his hand to lift the heavy door knocker when a small door cut out of one wing of the great door of Palazzo Lo Mascolo opened and out came Doctor Bellanca, medical bag in hand.

"I've been here all morning, which is why I couldn't come to the club," he said, shaking don Anselmo's hand. "How'd it turn out?"

"The request was deemed invalid."

"So much the better," said the doctor, and he started to close the small door behind him.

"Please leave it open," said don Anselmo.

"Do you want to go in?"

He'd asked the question without budging a single millimeter from the doorway, so that don Anselmo couldn't get by him.

"Yes."

"Did you want to see the baron?"

What was with all the questions?

"Yes."

The doctor closed the small door decisively.

"He's in no condition to receive you, believe me."

Don Anselmo balked. So the baron really was sick after all!

"Is it anything serious?"

"Well, yes and no."

"Does he have the flu? . . . "

"No, it's not the flu."

"Then what's wrong with him?"

Bellanca seemed a little uneasy.

"It's . . . how shall I say? An unusual case."

"Oh, well. I'll just go and say hello to the baroness and—"

"She can't receive you, either."

"She's caught it too?"

"Well . . . yes, in a manner of speaking."

"What about *Baronessina* Antonietta?"

Dr. Bellanca made a strange face.

"Well, let's just say she . . . is the origin of the illness."

How could that be? The baronessina was an eighteen-year-old girl as beautiful as the sun and more bursting with health than even her father!

"Listen, doctor. If this illness spreads so easily . . . "

"Please don't be alarmed, and, most importantly, don't go spreading the word. You mustn't needlessly stoke people's fears. The baron and his family are in a kind of quarantine in there. They need only avoid direct contact with others. In a few days it'll all be over."

Don Anselmo remembered he'd shaken Bellanca's hand. He shuddered. He was deathly afraid of illness.

"Er, doctor, did you by any chance wash your hands?"

Without answering, Bellanca walked away cursing. As he began to head home, don Anselmo turned around to look at Palazzo Lo Mascolo. All the shutters over the windows and balconies were closed. As if the family were in mourning. There was no visible sign of life inside. At one o'clock on a Sunday afternoon? With a sun hot enough to split rocks? What, were they all dead or something?

To go home, don Anselmo had no choice but to walk past Palazzo Cammarata, which stood all by itself on a street that was also called Cammarata. Nobility dictated that the palazzo mustn't have any other constructions around it. The great house took up the whole street and had only its private garden, the *firriato*, in front.

Reaching the end of the street, which led into Piazza Unità d'Italia, don Anselmo stopped and looked around in bewilderment. Something had unnerved him at Palazzo Cammarata, but he couldn't figure out what it was.

The silence! That's what it was!

Marquis Filadelfo head eight daughters, the youngest being five years old and the oldest eighteen, a wife—Marquise Ernestina—who was vociferous by nature, and two maids. The only man amidst eleven women who were always quarreling one minute, laughing the next, crying one minute, chattering the next, cursing each other one moment, raising hell the next, the marquis would sometimes lose his head, and the nervous agitation from which he suffered even while asleep would become so great that he would go outside dressed just as he was and, to let off steam, pick a fight with the first person he passed on the street. Everything that went on inside the palazzo always became instantly known to whoever happened to be walking along Via Cammarata. The chatter of the eleven women, who habitually spoke loudly, would waft out of the windows, which were perpetually open, rain or shine, bounce off the stones outside and back into the windows through which it had just exited.

So, why was the palazzo now as silent as the grave? Looking up, don Anselmo noticed that all the shutters over the windows were closed, something he'd never seen before. What could have happened?

"No, no, no . . . " he said to himself. "They're not playing straight with me here, neither the baron nor the marquis!"

And he turned and went back, determined to knock on the door and demand an explanation. But after he'd taken barely three steps, he froze.

Breathlessly approaching from the other end of the street was Dr. Bellanca, with his medical bag in hand.

"Were you going to the marquis's?"

"Yes."

"Did he send for you?"

"No, but as I was passing by I noticed—"

"Please, don Anselmo, just go home."

"But why?"

"Because I don't think the marquis is in any condition to see you," said the doctor, knocking at the door.

"Is he sick?"

"Yes."

"But I saw him at the club this morning!"

"That doesn't mean anything. The . . . er . . . In short, it came on all of a sudden."

The explanation dawned on don Anselmo, as sudden and swift as a punch in the stomach.

"Accompanied by diarrhea?" he asked in terror.

"Among other things."

"*O matre santissima!* So it's an epidemic!"

The great door came open and the doctor went inside. The door then closed again.

For the second time, don Anselmo asked himself what was two plus two.

And he answered his own question. And "four," this time, could equal only one terrible thing: cholera. There'd been a wave of cholera a few years back that had ushered half of the town into the cemetery. He stood there staring at the closed windows for a moment; then, leaning even more on his cane, since his legs were trembling more than usual, he walked quickly home, opened the door, went in, sat down in a chair in the vestibule, and was unable to go any further.

His wife, Signura Agata, who'd heard the door open, came out into the vestibule and saw her husband there, looking as pale as a corpse and fanning his face with his hat. She got worried.

"'Nzelmù, what happened? Are you unwell? Why do you look like that, eh?"

"Just be quiet for a minute and let me catch my breath, dammit!"

But the signura couldn't restrain herself.

"Talk to me, 'Nzelmù, you're frightening me! *Matre santa*, what's wrong?"

"Nothing's wrong! And stop buzzing around me like some kind of mosquito! Where's Girolamu?"

"The coachman? I don't know."

"Tell the maid to go and find him. I want him to hitch up the big carriage."

"Why? Are you going somewhere? May I ask where?"

"Agatì, you're coming with me, and we're leaving straight away."'

"What! And where are we going?"

"To the country!"

"Back to San Giusippuzzo? We were there less than a week ago!"

"And now I feel like going back, devil take it all!"

"All right, all right, there's no need to curse. But how long will we stay?"

"I figure about a month."

"What! So long? Why?"

"Agatì, there's something going on in town I don't like the look of. Baron Lo Mascolo's whole family is sick, all of 'em, and everyone in Palazzo Cammarata's sick too."

"The flu's been going around."

"What flu? The main thing that's going around is Doctor Bellanca! And the bastard won't tell me anything! But I figured it out all by myself. There's an epidemic, Agatì! Maybe cholera!"

"*Matre tutta santa e biniditta!* I'll go and start packing the trunks!"

They left two hours later, and it took the usual hour to reach San Giusippuzzo. The road was in such bad shape that several times the carriage very nearly fell into a ditch. Finally, by the grace of God, Girolamu halted the two horses inside the enclosure that contained the Buttafavas' villa, the wine vat, the stables, the carriage house, and the cottage of 'Ngilino the overseer, who lived there with his wife Catarina and daughter of seventeen, Totina. From the window of his coach, don Anselmo noticed that there didn't seem to be anyone in the house, since the door as well as all the shutters were closed.

Since the overseer hadn't been expecting his masters' arrival, he must surely be out in the fields somewhere. And

Catarina and Totina must have gone into town, since it was Sunday.

Don Anselmo climbed down from the carriage and went and opened the front door of the villa. As his wife was going inside, he said to his coachman:

"Try calling 'Ngilino. If he's somewhere nearby, he can help you bring the trunks inside."

The master bedroom was upstairs. Don Anselmo lay down with all his clothes on; the journey had worn him out and, on top of that, he hadn't been able to have his usual afternoon nap.

"I'm going to have a little rest," he said to his wife, who was bustling from room to room.

He fell asleep at once and slept for two straight hours.

*

He was awakened by Signura Agata, his wife.

"Time to wake up. Girolamu and 'Ngilino are bringing up the trunk with the clothes."

He went into the privy.

When he reemerged, his wife was taking the clothes out of the trunk, and he could tell she was angry because she was whining with her mouth closed. Agata was a good-hearted woman, but she liked to be served. She normally wouldn't even bend down to pick up a pin that had fallen to the floor.

"What need is there for you to do that work yourself? You could have asked Catarina and Totina to do it when they got back from town."

"'Ngilino told me they didn't go into town."

"Then where did they go?"

"They didn't go anywhere. They're right here, at home."

"At home? Then why didn't they come out when we arrived?"

"Because they're sick."

"Both of 'em?"

"Both of 'em."

"But were they in church this morning?"

At don Anselmo's personal request, Don Ernesto Pintacuda, priest of the church of Saints Cosma and Damiano, had accepted Catarina and Totina as members of his parish, when they should by rights have gone to the church of the Most Holy Crucifix, the peasants' church. The fact of the matter was that don Ansemlo was terribly fond of Totina. The girl was a sight to behold, and her cheerful disposition was contagious. Don Anselmo would sometimes spend hours out on the balcony, watching the girl performing her chores in the farmyard. And, unbeknownst to Signura Agata, he'd even given her money to buy herself some nice clothes so she would look good at Sunday Mass.

"No, they weren't."

A thought flashed into don Anselmo's mind.

"Shit!"

"What's with you?"

"Shit shit shit!"

"Don't use obscenities! What's wrong?"

"The clo . . . the locked doors! The closed windows! Just like Palazzo Lo Mascolo! And . . . and Palazzo Cammarata! Put all the clothes back in the trunk!"

"Have you lost your mind?"

"Agatì! The epi . . . the epidemic has spread here too!"

He went out of the room, raced down the stairs and into the courtyard, headed for the stables, went upstairs, and promptly kicked open the door to the room where the coachman slept.

Girolamu, who was in his underpants, very nearly had a heart attack.

"Wha—what is it, sir?"

"Hitch the carriage back up! We're leaving!"

"Where to, sir?"

"To La Forcaiola!"

Girolamu looked bewildered.

"But, sir, that'll take a two and a half hours at the very least! And it'll be dark soon."

"I don't give a damn. Hitch 'em up! Then come and get the trunks!"

"Could I ask 'Ngilino to give me a hand, sir?"

"No! You mustn't so much as look at his shadow!"

"Sir, can I tell you something, since your missus isn't present?"

"Tell me."

"You should know that people are saying Salamone the brigand's been hanging around Forcaiola way."

That was all they needed! Salamone the brigand not only stripped any nobleman or bourgeois he encountered of everything he had, leaving him as naked as Adam, but he never passed on any woman he crossed paths with either. He did them all, from age fifteen to fifty, right before the eyes of their husbands, fathers, and brothers, whom his henchmen would restrain. Anselmo's wife was already past sixty, and so wasn't in any danger.

The problem was that Salamone was liable to make off with the carriage itself, leaving both of them—actually, all three of them, since the brigand certainly wouldn't spare even Girolamu—naked on a godforsaken country road in the middle of the night.

But, between cholera and the brigand, the choice was clear.

"Hitch 'em up! Hitch 'em up!"

*

La Forcaiola was an estate belonging to a first cousin of don Anselmo, don Lovicino Scattola, who at present was in prison in Palermo, serving a seven-year term for having killed don Michelangelo Fichera during a hunting party, after the latter had claimed, just minutes before, that don Lovicino had never in all his life managed to shoot a rabbit or hare because he was incapable of hitting even an elephant from two feet away. And so don Lovicino shot him from thirty feet away, just to show, in the presence of witnesses, that the man was wrong.

Upon hearing news of his boss's sentence, Benuzzo Cogliastro, don Lovicino's farm overseer, had felt his heart fill with joy. For seven years he would be the real owner of the estate. But then one day don Anselmo had shown up with full power of attorney granted by his cousin, and Benuzzo had sworn to get even with him. For this reason don Anselmo didn't show his face much around there, if at all, and only went when he absolutely had to. As in the present instance.

*

They arrived late at night, luckily without having crossed paths with Salamone the brigand. The situation at the estate was almost exactly the same as at San Giusippuzzo. The shutters of Benuzzo's house seemed to be open, but there wasn't a hint of any light inside. Surely the whole family was asleep. Girolamu took the cart lamp out out from under the carriage and lit the way for don Anselmo, who was holding the keys, to unlock the main door of the villa. Signura Agata hadn't wanted to get out of the carriage before the all the oil lamps in the entrance hall were lit.

Hands trembling from fatigue, don Anselmo had to try three times before successfully putting the key into the door. And at that exact moment, a rifle shot rang out, splitting his eardrums. The large boarshot of the *lupara* blasted several holes in the great door, just a few inches from his head. And the two horses, frightened by the blast, started running towards the farmyard exit, with Signura Agata screaming wildly. But when the animals took a turn a little too sharply, the left wheel crashed against the wall and the carriage flipped.

"I'm dying!" cried Signura Agata, before fainting.

"Get out of here or I'll kill you all!" a man shouted angrily.

Don Anselmo, dropping to the ground and shaking in terror, recognized the voice of Benuzzo, the farm manager.

"Benuzzo! It's me, don Anselmo! Don't shoot!"

By way of reply a flash went off in one of the windows of Benuzzo's house, and don Anselmo closed his eyes.

"I'm a dead man!" he thought.

The shot hit the great door again.

"You're not don Anselmo, you're Salamone the brigand and you take me for a fool!" said Benuzzo.

"Get me out of here! Help! Somebody get me out of here!" Signura Agata shouted in the meantime, having regained consciousness.

Since Girolamu had dropped the cart lamp in terror and was now spread out belly-down on the ground, praying to the Madonna aloud, don Anselmo got a crazy idea.

He reached out, grabbed the lamp, and held it next to his face.

"Take a good look at me, you stupid shit! I'm don Anselmo!"

"Oh! So it's you? I din't rec'nize you, sorry. You coulda told me you was comin'! I'll be right down."

At that moment don Anselmo realized, from Benuzzo's tone of voice, that the overseer had known perfectly well from the moment the carriage had entered the courtyard that it was him and not Salamone the brigand.

And he'd shot at him on purpose, the bastard!

But when he tried to stand up, don Anselmo was unable. His body ached all over.

"Go and help the signora!" he yelled at Girolamu.

By this point the voices of the farmer's wife Ciccina, son

Paolino, and daughter Michilina could be heard inside the house, as they hurriedly got dressed to go and help the masters who had just arrived.

Benuzzo came down out of breath and, with a lamp in his hand, bent down to look at don Anselmo. He still had his rifle in his other hand.

"Wha'd I do, hit you?"

"No."

"Well, I'm glad for that! Here, lemme help you up."

And he held out his hand. Don Anselmo didn't take it at once, but instead asked Benuzzo a strange question:

"Everyone in the family all right?"

"Everyone's fine, thanks be to God."

Only then did don Anselmo grasp the farm manager's hand. If they were all fine, it meant that the cholera, luckily, hadn't spread to that area yet.

Chapter III
Don Anselmo's Cholera and Other Complications

At around the same time that don Anselmo finally managed to fall asleep at La Forcaiola—that is, around four in the morning—the great door of Palazzo Lo Mascolo was carefully opened, and a man's head poked out and looked both ways to make sure there wasn't anyone around.

Reassured, the man came out, closing the door behind him.

He was completely masked, wearing a cloak tossed over his left shoulder in such a way that it covered his face, leaving only the eyes visible, since the beret on his head was pulled down over his brow.

On his feet the man had an old pair of hobnailed boots like the kind the peasants wore. In his right hand he was holding a shepherd's staff.

Walking away, he didn't encounter another living soul. But even if he had seen someone, the person was unlikely to recognize that bundled-up peasant as Baron don Fofò Lo Mascolo.

Arriving at the home of Teresi the lawyer, a lone, freestanding house near the top of the hill whose slopes the town was built on—indeed behind the lawyer's house was a drop of some two hundred feet—the baron stopped, raised his walking stick, and knocked hard on the wooden door. Nobody came to open it.

Teresi was not married, and lived with a lad of twenty, Stefano Pillitteri, son of his sister, who had married a ne'er-do-well and died young. The lawyer was very fond of his intelligent nephew and kept him around as an apprentice, paying for him to study law at the University of Palermo.

The baron resumed his assault. As he was slamming the

knocker with all his might with his right hand, he rapped his cane against the door with his left, all the while kicking the door with his hobnailed boots. You could have opened a tomb with all the racket he was making. And, indeed, through the shutter slats over one of the upstairs windows a dim light came on, the window opened, and Teresi the lawyer appeared, reciting his customary formula:

"My door is open to everyone. Therefore, whoever you are, you are welcome in this house. I'll be right down to open the door."

Five minutes later, the man entered the house. At first Teresi didn't recognize him. But as soon as the man removed his barracan and cap, the lawyer balked in surprise.

"Baron! So it's you? Why are you dressed like that?"

"I didn't want anyone to recognize me."

"Why not? You've certainly never put on a disguise to come to my house before."

"Well, this time I did."

"Let's go into my study."

Teresi sat down behind the desk, while the baron settled into the armchair opposite it.

"Shall I make some coffee?"

"No."

There was a silent pause. The lawyer knew from experience that it was always best to let the person in front of you make the first move.

"Is your nephew here?" the baron asked after a spell.

"Stefano? Yes, he's in his room, sleeping."

"And why didn't he wake up?"

"No idea. Maybe because kids sleep deeply. May I ask why you came here at this hour of the night?"

"To kill your nephew Stefano," said Baron Lo Mascolo, taking a revolver out of his pocket and setting it down on the desk. "Shall we wake him up?"

*

Signura Agata, meanwhile, had confided to her chambermaid Suntina the reason why they were in such a hurry to get away from Palizzolo.

"My husband don Anselmo says it looks like there's cholera going around. But he doesn't want anyone to know."

The last time cholera had passed through town, Suntina had lost her father, mother, all four grandparents and her only brother. Afterwards, she was taken in by her father's brother, Tamazio, a peasant who ended up treating her like a servant (which was normal), deflowered her at age thirteen (which was also normal), but also demanded that the girl wash his feet every Sunday. This was not normal, and Suntina would not stand for it. So she ran away and knocked at the first door she saw. Which was the front door of Palazzo Lobue, where lived Galatina and Natale Lobue, Agata's young parents. Suntina helped raise the little girl, and when Agata got married to don Anselmo, she brought Suntina with her.

"Do you want to come with us, Suntì?"

"No, ma'am. I'd rather stay here and wait for you to come back."

"But that may be dangerous, you know."

"I know, but if I stay, I can watch the house for you."

And this was a good idea, since during the last wave of cholera many houses had been robbed and ransacked.

"As you wish."

As soon as the masters had left, Giseffa, the other housekeeper, who wasn't yet twenty years old, went into such a song and dance that Suntina was forced to tell her the reason for their departure.

"*Matre santa!* Cholera! I'm leaving too! Right now!" said Giseffa, scared out of her wits.

"And where you gonna go?"

"To my father's house."

"But your father's house is also here in town! Listen to me: just stay here, that would be best."

"Why would that be best?"

"First, because cholera never attacks the rich, only the poor. If we stay here, in the house of rich people, it's possible that when the cholera passes through it'll be in a hurry and mistake us for rich people too. Secondly, because here there's flour, cheese, salted sardines, tomatoes, and all the water we need. We could hole up here for at least three months without ever having to go out. We'll lock the great door and not open for anyone."

"No. I want to go to my father's house."

"Listen, tell you what. Since don Anselmo doesn't want the news of the cholera to get out right away, you'll sleep here tonight, and tomorrow morning, you can get up at the crack of dawn and go to your father."

"Is this some kind of joke, Baron?"

"I'm warning you, Teresi, if you piss me off, I'll shoot you too."

"All right, all right. But can you at least tell me the reason?"

"Shall we set something straight, first?"

"If you think we need to, then yes, of course."

"How would you characterize the relations you and I have always had?"

"I would say they've always been good."

"And I would say excellent. I'll cite just one example. Didn't I entrust you with my lawsuit against Baron Mostocotto instead of giving it to the lawyer Moschino, who was very keen on having it?"

The reason for the dispute between the two barons was that one day, Baron Mostocotto, who had a weak bladder and therefore was always having to pee, was caught by don Fofò urinating against a corner of Palazzo Lo Mascolo. The baron took umbrage.

"Look," Mostocotto had said to him, to defuse the situation, "if you want some kind of compensation, you can come and pee on my palazzo whenever you like."

But there was no settling the dispute, not even with the authoritative intervention of Giallonardo the notary. Baron Lo Mascolo finally sued his fellow baron for damages to his building.

"Yes, that's true," Teresi admitted.

"And didn't I pay you, with no questions asked, the rather considerable advance you asked of me?"

"Yes, sir, you did."

"And when you asked me to support your request for membership to the club, did I support you or not?"

"Of course you did."

"And did I not allow your nephew, Stefano, to come and call at our house whenever he liked?"

"Yes. And I am very grateful to you for your generosity."

"But he's not."

"I'm sorry, he who?"

"Your nephew."

"He hasn't been grateful to you?"

"No."

"And that's why you want to shoot him?"

"Stop speaking twaddle, Teresi."

"Then why?"

"Three days ago, my daughter Antonietta felt unwell. For the first time in eighteen years. And so my wife sent for Dr. Bellanca. Ever since, my house has been in deep mourning."

"Oh my God, is her illness really so serious?"

"Serious? My daughter is dead!"

The lawyer stood up.

"Please allow me to embrace you, Baron," he said sincerely. "So terrible a misfortune warrants—"

"Just remain seated or a terrible misfortune will befall you instead. Until tonight, despite my wife's prayers, my daughter hadn't wanted to talk about it."

Teresi broke into a cold sweat. Baron Lo Mascolo had surely lost his mind; there could be no other explanation. One branch of that family did have a history of madness. Hadn't the baron's sister, donna Romilda, become a nun? And hadn't she one fine day, after twenty years of cloistered life, come out of the convent and start dancing naked?

"Well, the problem, my dear baron, is that, normally, we can pray all we want, but the dead don't—"

"What dead?"

Teresi wiped the sweat from his brow with one hand.

"Baron, unless I'm mistaken, just a moment ago you told me your daughter was dead, and so—"

"For me, she's dead. For her mother, she's not."

So had the baroness lost her mind too? Both husband and wife, stark raving mad? That sort of thing does happen sometimes, in families. Didn't Signura Rossitano think she was a wasp and her husband a hornet, and they communicated by buzzing?

"Listen, Baron, maybe you'd better go home and—"

"I'll go home after I've shot your nephew."

This time Teresi snapped. He was fed up.

"Would you please be so kind as to tell me why the hell you want to kill Stefano? What's he got to do with this whole business?"

"He's got everything to do with it. He's the only person who could have made my daughter Antonietta pregnant."

*

Giseffa the maid arrived at her father's house in Vicolo Raspa as the town-hall belfry was ringing four o'clock in the morning. At 4:05 A.M., Giseffa's mother, Nunziata, opened the window and started shouting:

"Cholera! Cholera!"

Since the street was narrow, her shouts were heard in all twenty-five of the residences situated on it. The first family to head out to the country were the Cumellas, then the Licatas, the Bonacciòs, the Gaglios, the Bonadonnas, the Restivos . . . In short, by five o'clock the only ones left in Vicolo Raspa were seven cats, two dogs, and Tano Pullara, who, being ninety years old, didn't feel like going anywhere with the others and said that he welcomed the cholera because he was tired of living.

At ten past five, Gesummino Torregrossa, who every morning on his way to work came by at five to pick up his friend, Girlanno Tumminia, found nobody at home and saw only Tano Pullara, sitting outside his hovel. He asked him what had happened.

"There's cholera about," said the old man.

"Says who?"

"Don Anselmo Buttafava."

Gesummino turned around and raced back to Vicolo Centostelle where he lived. By five-thirty, half of that street, too, was empty.

At the day's first Mass, at six A.M., the priests all seemed to have spread the word among themselves.

Faces that had never been seen in the churches before suddenly appeared: servants, coachmen, stable boys, hard laborers, wet nurses, housemaids, cooks from the noble houses, had all sat themselves down beside their masters, and all were praying to the little lord Jesus to save them from cholera.

Then there were the people just passing through who were ready to run away to the countryside but first wanted the Lord's blessing. But in the various different churches, three families were noticeably absent: those of don Anselmo Buttafava, Marquis Cammarata, and Baron Lo Mascolo.

It's a well-known fact that there's no sermon at the day's first Mass.

And yet on this occasion the priests all stepped up to their pulpits, but, instead of preaching the sermon, they hurled insults and curses.

Patre Eriberto Raccuglia warned:

"Didn't I tell you that this town would end up like Sodom and Gomorrah? You must drive out the devil, who has taken the form of Teresi the lawyer . . . "

Patre Alessio Terranova said:

"It's no use crying and beseeching God to save you from cholera! First you must free the town!"

Patre Filiberto Cusa exclaimed:

"The poison plant must be uprooted!"

Patre Alighiero Scurria scoffed:

"So now you're crying, eh? So now you're praying, eh? You're all a bunch of sheep crawling on all fours! And what did you do when I told you Teresi was the devil incarnate? Nothing! But maybe there's still time . . . "

Patre Libertino Samonà proclaimed:

"It's time to embark on a holy crusade!"

Patre Angelo Marrafà threatened:

"I swear that no survivors of the cholera shall ever set foot again in this church if they haven't first got rid of Matteo Teresi!"

Patre Ernesto Pintacuda heroically offered his services:

"I'll lead the charge and hold the Cross high!"

Only Patre Mariano Dalli Cardillo didn't preach that day. He limited himself to praying, along with his flock, for the Lord to save them all from the cholera looming at the city gates like a terrible scourge.

*

The mayor, Nicolò Calandro, was woken up by a great deal of shouting under his windows. His wife, Filippa, who was as deaf as a doorpost, kept right on sleeping. He immediately thought it was something he'd been fearing would happen sooner or later: a popular uprising unleashed by that incorrigible sonofabitch, Matteo Teresi.

And he imagined himself strung up, head down, from the tree in the middle of the public garden, as had happened thirty years earlier to his predecessor, Mayor Bonifazi.

"They'll never take me alive!" he shouted, getting out of bed and grabbing the revolver he kept in the drawer of his nightstand.

Barefoot as he was, and still in his nightshirt, he went up to the window and looked through the shutters, which luckily were not fully closed.

He was flabbergasted to see what he saw.

An endless stream of men, women, old folks, youngsters, and children leading a procession of goats, sheep, chickens, and rabbits, running along as they pulled small handcarts or an occasional donkey with household objects piled on top, mattresses, cooking pots, water jugs, chests filled with clothing . . .

But it wasn't a revolution. They were not angry at him. The people were fleeing. But why? What was happening in town? He opened the shutter, stuck his head out, and asked:

"What on earth is going on?"

"Cholera! Cholera!" said many voices as one.

What the hell were they saying? Cholera?

"Who told you there was cholera?"

"Don Anselmo Buttafava," said a woman's voice.

Don Anselmo was generally considered a sensible person, and should therefore be taken at his word. But then why hadn't Dr. Bellanca said anything about it to him, the mayor?

Mayor Calandro got dressed in a flash and went out of the house without bothering to wake his wife. Five minutes later he was knocking on the doctor's door.

A window opened.

"My husband's gone out looking for you, Mr. Mayor," Signura Bellanca said from the window.

City Hall was still closed at that hour, which meant that the doctor must be headed for the mayor's house. And in fact he found him there at the door, knocking pointlessly, since Signura Filippa's deafness was so great she would even miss an earthquake.

"Why didn't you tell me there was cholera about?" the mayor asked angrily.

"Calm down! And don't speak to me in that tone of voice!"

"But aren't you aware of my responsibilities as mayor of this town?"

"Of course!"

"So why didn't you tell me anything about the cholera? It's obviously been festering for days, and you—"

"Oh, enough of this cholera nonsense!" the doctor interrupted him.

The mayor thought he'd heard wrong.

"What did you say? You mean there's no cholera?"

"Precisely! Just to be safe, before coming here, I went and woke up my colleague, Dr. Palumbo, and he too was taken completely by surprise."

"So then how do you explain that don Anselmo Buttafava . . . "

People kept streaming past them at a run. One of them, holding a sickle in his hand, stopped.

"So you rich folk aren't running away, eh? Cholera never attacks you bastards!"

"Get out of here or I'll kill you!" shouted the mayor, pulling out the revolver he'd put in his pocket.

A woman grabbed the man by the arm and pulled him away with her.

"Don't go getting into trouble, Ninù," she said.

"Bastards!"

"I can explain what happened," the doctor said as soon as the man was gone, "but not in the middle of the street like this, with all these people around. It's a very confidential thing."

"Let's go to City Hall."

But after they'd taken just a few steps they were hailed by Totò Carrubba, who had a little food shop. The man was pulling his hair out in despair.

"They're cleaning me out! I'm ruined!"

"What happened, Totò?" asked the mayor.

"They broke down the door of my shop! They're stealing everything."

So now there was looting? Calandro made a snap decision.

"Doctor, you can tell me about don Anselmo later. We need some law and order here! I have to go and talk to the carabinieri."

*

"My good baron, let me remind you, before you enter my nephew's bedroom, that you gave me your word of honor that you would not shoot him before I've had a chance to talk to him."

"And I will keep my word."

They went in. The lad was sleeping like a baby. Teresi was holding an oil lamp, the baron his revolver. Firmly convinced of his nephew's innocence, the lawyer was extremely tense and ready to throw the oil lamp in the baron's face the moment the latter made any move to start shooting.

Teresi approached the bed, while don Fofò, in keeping with the agreement they'd come to in the lawyer's study after two hours of negotiation, stood fast in the doorway.

"Stefanù, wake up," said Teresi, shaking the young man's shoulder.

The nephew opened his eyes and immediately shielded them with his arm, as the lamp was right in front of his face

"What time is it anyway?" he asked in a hoarse voice.

"I don't know. Six-thirty, seven o'clock . . . "

"Has something happened?"

And he made as if to get up. But if he got out of bed, he would surely notice the baron.

"Stay in bed. I just need to ask you something."

"So ask."

"Do you swear you'll tell me the truth?"

"Of course!"

"Swear on your mother's soul?"

"I swear on my mother's soul. What do you want to know?"

Teresi swallowed and then spat out the question in a loud voice, so the baron could hear him clearly.

"Did you do anything with the daughter of Baron Lo Mascolo?"

"With Antonietta? Do what?"

Teresi was worried that if he said even one wrong word, the baron might feel offended and start firing wildly. And he ended up doing even worse.

"Do 'it.'"

And just so as not to be mistaken, he made a fist and pumped it back and forth.

"Know what I mean?"

But then, realizing the gesture he'd just made without thinking, he closed his eyes and waited for a bullet to shatter his skull.

CHAPTER IV
WHAT DR. BELLANCA TOLD MAYOR CALANDRO

The lad reacted with unexpected violence, his right hand shooting straight out of from under the cover and striking his uncle's left cheek hard.

"Don't you ever dare say anything like that about Antonietta."

He was now sitting up in bed, trembling with indignation and white as a sheet.

"You must tell me who it was who said those vile things about her! I'll kill him with my bare hands!"

Teresi, who as a lawyer had a way with words, was suddenly speechless. To his immense satisfaction, and despite his burning cheek, he was becoming acquainted with his nephew's true nature, which until that moment had remained hidden.

"Calm down, Stefanù!" he managed to say.

"No, I won't calm down! You must tell me who told you that calumny!"

There was no longer any reason for the baron to remain in the shadows outside the door.

"*Signor barone*, please, if you will . . . "

There was no reply.

"The baron is here?" Stefano asked in shock.

Without answering, Teresi stood up, went out of the room, and managed just in time to see don Fofò opening the front door to go outside.

"*Signor barone!*"

Don Fofò turned around, looked at him, stood there in silence for a moment, then said:

'"Your nephew convinced me."

And he left, closing the door behind him.

Teresi had just turned round to go back to his nephew's bedroom when he again heard knocking at the door, accompanied by kicks and cane-blows, just like a few hours earlier.

It could only be the baron again, newly prey to the whims of his folly.

"Somebody's knocking," Stefano said from his room.

Teresi didn't move. He didn't know what to do. Wasn't it too dangerous to let that raging madman back into the house?

"Please open the door, for Christ's sake, they're coming!" said the baron from outside the door.

And who could it be that was coming? Surely these were fantasies that existed only in the baron's fevered brain. At any rate, weighing his options, Teresi decided it was best to find out what was going on.

"Stefanù, look out the window and tell me if you see any people coming."

He heard the window opening, followed by the frightened voice of his nephew.

"There's hundreds of them!"

But who the hell were all these people coming? Since the baron clearly was not seeing ghosts but real people in the flesh, Teresi raced downstairs and opened the door for him. Don Fofò rushed in, out of breath and panting.

"They're on their way here!"

"But *who* is on their way here?"

"How the hell should I know? Men and women armed with clubs, pitchforks, and hoes and being led by a priest carrying a cross! I don't want them to recognize me!"

"But what do they want?"

"How the hell should I know?" the baron repeated, more alarmed than ever.

At that moment they heard the first shouts.

"Death to Teresi! Death to the devil incarnate!"

"Give me your revolver and come with me," said the lawyer, who had turned white as a sheet.

At the back of the entrance hall was a window that Teresi opened. The morning light poured in.

"You can go out this way."

"But there's an overhang!"

"No, that's what it looks like, but there's a very narrow pathway that leads down below. You just need to be a little careful."

Closing the window, Teresi went into his study, took his revolver, and when upstairs. Stefano looked as if he was in a daze and no longer understood what was going on. His uncle handed him the baron's gun.

"If they try to break down the door, fire a shot from your window. But in the air, first time around. I mean it. If they don't run away, get back inside and shut yourself up. I'm going into my room."

But there weren't hundreds of them. There were about sixty, which was quite enough to do damage. At that moment they were all kneeling, and the priest with the cross was giving them benediction.

"O my holy crusaders," he said. "You, my beloved children, who revere the sanctity of the family and keep watch over the virtues of the home . . . "

Taking advantage of the fact that they were all looking at the priest, Teresi opened the shutters slowly, just enough to slip his hand with the revolver out the window.

Then, all at once, the priest, whom Teresi recognized as Patre Raccuglia, turned around, raised the cross in the air, and said:

"Go! Let's rid ourselves of the demon!"

In a flash Teresi realized these people would break down the door on their first try.

"Shoot!" he shouted to Stefano, as he did the same.

The echoes of the two shots hadn't yet faded before there

was nobody left in front of the house. Or, at least, there was nobody still standing. Because there were in fact a man and a woman lying on the ground.

Teresi felt his blood run cold. But he'd shot up into the air! He was positive! He ran into his nephew's bedroom.

"I told you to shoot in the air!"

"I did!"

They looked back outside. The man, by now, had stood up, and the woman was getting to her feet. They'd fainted in fear and were now running away.

At around eight o'clock that morning, the marshal of the Palizzolo Carabinieri station, Vitangelo Sciabbarrà, in direct consultation with the mayor, declared that the situation was worsening.

Indeed three shops had already been looted; some burglars had tried to enter Palazzo Spartà before they were driven away by a pair of rifle blasts fired by don Liborio and his wife Vetusta, who was the best shot in town; and there had been an attempted assault on the Veronica brothers' mill.

The brothers had also defended themselves with rifles, with one fatality. True, the victim was a delinquent with five or six burglary convictions already; but he was still dead.

What was happening was that many men, having accompanied their families out to the country, had come back into town to take advantage of the situation and steal what there was to be stolen.

The mayor was normally supposed to have six municipal policemen at his disposal, but hadn't seen a single one of them that morning. No doubt they had all run away. And what could the ten carabinieri at the station do by themselves? At half past eight, Marshal Sciabbarrà phoned the main headquarters at Camporeale, which was some twenty kilometers away, to ask for reinforcements.

And by twelve-thirty the reinforcements arrived, in the form of a squadron of mounted carabinieri under the command of Captain Eugenio Montagnet, who declared martial law and took over all local operations.

At two o'clock that afternoon, a half-witted wretch who got by on begging for alms and whose name nobody could really remember, since everyone knew him only as *'u cani* (that is, "the dog"), was "made to suffer the consequences" after being caught with a kilo of potatoes without being able to explain where he'd got them. Nobody witnessed the execution. Twelve carabinieri shot him against the wall of the ancient convent. *'U cani* died laughing, convinced up to the very end that it was all some kind of joke, one of the many that the townfolk were always playing on him for their amusement.

By four o'clock that afternoon, absolute calm reigned in Palizzolo.

At half past four, Captain Montagnet had an idea: to send his men into the countryside to inform those who had run away that there was no danger of cholera and they could therefore safely return to town.

"I don't think your soldiers will have any success convincing them," said the mayor.

"Why not?" asked Montagnet.

"Because they're carabinieri," replied the mayor.

"Shall we make a bet?" said the captain.

Then, turning to a reed-thin lieutenant by the name of Villasevaglios who was always at his side, he said:

"They'll be under your command. And don't make me lose that bet."

"Yessir!" said the lieutenant, snapping to attention.

And he left the room. The captain turned towards the mayor, lighting a cigar.

"I've heard a report that this morning there was an

attempted attack on the home of a lawyer whose name I can't remember . . . "

"Teresi."

"Yes, right. Apparently this lawyer, along with a relative of his, fired on the attackers. Is that true?"

"Well, in a sense . . . "

"Mr. Mayor, is it true or not?"

"It's true. But, you see, this lawyer—"

"Is it also true that the attackers were led by a priest brandishing a large cross?"'

"So I've been told. But, you see, for quite some time, this lawyer—"

"Would you please be so kind as to tell me this priest's name?"

How was he going to lie to him? By telling him he didn't know his name? This captain was jovial and polite, but he seemed to have a chip on his shoulder the size of Mount Etna. If he didn't answer the man's question, he was liable to be made to "suffer the consequences" like that poor wretch *'u cani*. The mayor took a deep breath.

"Don Eriberto Raccuglia, priest of the parish of the Mother Church."

"Listen, I would like to avoid any malicious gossip or speculation . . . Could you summon this priest here to City Hall at nine o'clock tomorrow morning?"

"Could *I* summon him? Why me?"

"Don't you see? If I have him taken to the carabinieri station, who knows what kind of reaction that would unleash."

The captain was right.

"All right."

"Thank you. And now would you please tell me who spread the rumor that there was cholera about, and why?"

Mayor Calandro broke into a cold sweat. If they started dragging the town's big cheeses into this mess, there could be serious complications.

"Apparently . . . it was all a very big misunderstanding."

"You think? So the public unrest was not, in your opinion, intentional?"

"I don't think so."

"That would be the second part."

The mayor felt flummoxed.

"I'm sorry, Captain, but the second part of what?"

"Of my question. You didn't answer the first part."

"And what was that?"

"The name of the person who started the rumor."

"To be honest . . . a few names were mentioned and until I am absolutely certain, you must understand that I—"

"We'll discuss this again in the morning," said Montagnet, rising to his feet. "Would you please tell me where this lawyer Teresi lives?"

This captain, the mayor thought bitterly, will end up doing more damage than the nonexistent cholera.

But the captain found no one at home at Teresi's.

After three full hours of discussion with his nephew, the lawyer had decided to go to Palazzo Lo Mascolo, to talk to the baron. He wanted an answer to a specific question: Was it Antonietta who had named Stefano as her lover, or was this just an idea don Fofò had got into his head? Stefano, who'd wanted to see the girl again, took him there in the tilbury.

But they never reached their destination.

To save time on their way into the center of town, they avoided the main road and took a sort of country trail that shortened the distance. There were no buildings or farms along this track, and hardly anyone ever took it. At the exact point where the trail crossed a road of beaten earth leading into the main square of the town, Stefano saw a large, fat sack in the middle of the path. He pulled on the horse's reins to avoid running over it.

"The sack is moving!" shouted Teresi.

Indeed, something inside the sack seemed to have shifted. They climbed down to have a look. The sack was closed with string wrapped several times around. Then they both heard, very faintly, a catlike sort of wail.

"There must be a cat in there," said Stefano.

"A cat the size of a tiger?" Teresi asked doubtfully.

Then he made up his mind. Pulling a hunting knife out from a pocket of his coat, he cut the string and opened the sack to empty it. Out came the blond head of a young man of about twenty, with his face so battered from punches and whacks that his eyes were little more than two fissures. Blood was running from his nose and ears. His lips were so swollen that his mouth looked like an open pomegranate. And past them they could see that his blood-filled mouth was missing three teeth. Clearly the young man had also been kicked in the face.

Teresi lowered the sack a bit more. The shoulders appeared. The young man was not a peasant. The clothes he was wearing, though tattered, were made of fine fabric.

"Do you know him?" Teresi asked his nephew.

"I think so."

"And who is he?"

"I think he's the son of a cousin of the Marquise Cammarata. He's not from around here, though he's often at the marquis's house. I met him at the ball on—"

"Fine, fine," said the lawyer, cutting him off. "Help me put him back in the sack."

"What?! He's a relative of the Cammaratas! We should take him to their palazzo and tell them how we found him and—"

"—And they'll just thank us and finish him off."

Stefano was dumbstruck.

"C'mon, give me a hand," said his uncle. "We'll take him to our house and then decide what to do."

"But let's at least take him out of the sack!"

"Not on your life. If we run across the carabinieri, they'll just think it's a sack of potatoes. Actually, let's do this. While I'm taking him home, you go and get Dr. Palumbo."

Teresi did not want to let this opportunity slip away. This kid was a relative of the Cammaratas. His lordship the marquis must surely know the reason for this brutal beating. His lordship! The great big son of a bitch who'd first supported his request for membership and then just dropped him. No, this was an opportunity not to be missed.

The very same people who were first to run away—the inhabitants of Vicolo Raspa, Giseffa included—got back into town around seven that evening, and Giseffa returned to the Buttafava home.

"You see? I won the bet! We managed to persuade them!" Captain Montagnet said in triumph to the mayor.

The carabinieri had indeed used the most persuasive of arguments: blows with the flat of their swords, lashes of the riding whip, and threats of arrest, all tactics in the subtle dialectics of the forces of order.

"May I come in? Am I bothering you?" asked Dr. Bellanca, poking his head into the mayor's office.

"No, quite the contrary, please sit down!" said Calandro.

"I've come to tell you how, in my opinion, don Anselmo was misled."

"You've come just in time."

"Why do you say that?"

"Because I believe that Captain Montagnet wants to charge him with disturbing the peace."

Bellanca couldn't hold back a curse.

"We really don't need this ball-busting captain at the moment!" he said.

"I agree," said the mayor. "And so, you wanted to tell me . . . "

"Could we close the door?"

"Is it a delicate matter?"

"Rather."

"I'll get it myself."

Before closing and locking the door, Calandro told the usher, who'd returned about an hour earlier after running away with two municipal policemen:

"Pippinè, I'm not here for anyone."

"Not even for the captain?"

"Especially not for the captain."

He went and sat back down in the armchair behind the desk and waited for his interlocutor to begin talking.

"Let me preface by saying that I am speaking to the mayor in my capacity as the municipal doctor."

"And so? What is that supposed to mean?"

"It means that I, as an ordinary doctor, would never tell you what I am about to tell you. But in my capacity as municipal doctor invested with an official responsibility, and faced with what happened in town today, I am forced to speak to you."

"So speak, for Christ's sake!"

"Three days ago," the doctor began, "I was summoned to an emergency at the home of Baron Lo Mascolo, when his daughter fell ill."

"Antonietta? She's the very picture of health! So what was she suffering from?"

"Maybe from too much health."

"I don't understand."

"She's pregnant."

"Pregnant?!"

"Two months pregnant."

"Two months pregnant?!"

"Antonietta."

"Antonietta?!"

"Would you please stop repeating everything I say? You're starting to get on my nerves."

"And do we know who the father is?"

"Antonietta didn't want to say. And I won't even go into what happened when I was forced to tell the baron and his wife that their daughter . . . Swoons, fainting fits, the baron going out of his mind and breaking chairs, vases, and anything else he could get his hands on . . . The following day, Sunday, I had to go back to give the baron some tranquilizers and the baroness some stimulants. But on my way out, I ran into don Anselmo. And that's when the trouble began."

"Why?"

"Because I couldn't very well tell don Anselmo the real reason I'd gone there. And so I answered his questions rather vaguely, and he ended up thinking I was treating something contagious."

"But that's a huge leap, from 'something contagious' to cholera!"

"Wait, I haven't finished. Right after leaving the baron's, I had to go back to Palazzo Cammarata."

"Go back to? You mean you'd been there earlier?"

"Yes indeed."

"When?"

"The day before."

"For what reason?"

"Their eldest daughter, Paolina, had taken ill."

Just from the doctor's expression, the mayor understood everything. He was in shock. He sat there for a moment with his mouth agape, then asked:

"Pregnant?"

"Pregnant."

"She too?"

"She too."

"Jesus bloody goddamn Christ!"

"I concur," said the doctor.

"How long?"

"Two months. Just like Antonietta."

"And Paolina doesn't want to say who the father is either?"

"She won't say a word."

"But how about these girls, anyway! All church and home and hearth, and suddenly they're all getting pregnant like nobody's business!"

"And, unfortunately," the doctor resumed, "as I was about to knock on the front door of Palazzo Cammarata, don Anselmo saw me and asked me whether somebody was sick in there. I said yes, and that was when he must have concluded that it was cholera."

"And now what are we going to tell our ball-busting captain?" asked the mayor. "If he discovers the truth, it's going to make the Sicilian Vespers look like a picnic!"

"I have an idea. For the good of the town—and also because I consider myself partly responsible for the misunderstanding—we'll have to lie."

"Meaning?"

"I could say that both the Lo Mascolo and Cammarata families came down with a particularly virulent form of influenza. And that was how don Anselmo got the wrong idea."

"Wait a second. But wasn't Marquis Cammarata at the club on Sunday morning?"

"We'll say that the poor man went just to be a good sport. That he was already sick on Sunday morning, but stubbornly refused to stay home and then got much sicker in the afternoon. As you can well imagine, neither the Lo Mascolos nor the Cammaratas would have any reason to want to contradict this story."

"Very well, then," said Calandro, expecting Bellanca to stand up.

But the doctor remained seated.

"Is there something else?" the mayor asked, starting to feel weary from a dreadful day.

"Yes, but I'm not sure it's relevant."

"To what?"

"To my public function."

"If you think it's something you should talk to me about, then talk, otherwise . . . "

"In short, we could consider even this a kind of epidemic," the doctor said, as though to himself.

"No, no," Calandro interjected, "if you think there really is an epidemic, then it is your duty to fill me in on it!"

"Do you know who the widow Cannata is?"

"How could I not? A fine-looking dame like that? And a serious, devout woman as well. Lost her husband three years ago, poor thing."

"Her too."

"I'm sorry, her too what?"

With his right hand, the doctor mimed a gesture indicating a large belly.

"Pregnant?!" the mayor asked in astonishment. "I don't believe it."

"You'd better believe it."

"Don't tell me she's two months pregnant!"

"I'm afraid I have to. And that's not all."

"It's not?"

"No. Do you know Totina, the daughter of 'Ngilino, don Anselmo's farm overseer?"

"Her too?"

"Yessirree, two months pregnant. And, like the widow Cannata, she doesn't want to reveal the father's name either."

"So, in all, there are four women who are presumably pregnant?"

"As far as I know. But it's possible my colleague Palumbo

knows of a few more. Though if there are any, he's not required, like me, to reveal their names."

The mayor sat there in thoughtful silence for a moment. Then he spoke.

"I don't think you can call it an epidemic. And, even it was one, how would we avoid its spread? Would we send the town crier out to warn all the woman to steer clear of all penises? Separate all the men from all the women? No, I really don't think so."

"I don't either. Also because nobody's ever heard of an epidemic of pregnancies," said the doctor.

*

At eleven o'clock that evening, a few of Captain Montagnet's carabinieri started making the rounds of the town's streets, announcing that the curfew would begin at twelve midnight sharp, that anyone who was found wandering outside after midnight would "suffer the consequences . . . "—*That captain is obsessed*, thought the mayor, who heard the announcement as he was on his way home—and that, in addition, all public assembly was prohibited until further notice.

Which meant, in plain language, that there would be no Masses, no classes at school, no markets in the square, and that even the Honor and Family Social Club would have to remain closed.

Finally, with God's help, at midnight what came to be known in Palizzolo as the day of don Anselmo's cholera came to an end.

The mayor got into bed beside his wife, Filippa, who was indeed deaf, but also young and pretty. But he didn't lie down. He remained sitting up, back propped against the pillows, and started counting on his fingers how many town hall employees were still absent.

"What are you counting?" asked Filppa. "When the last time we made love was? Well, you can stop counting, 'cause I can tell you myself. The last time was exactly two months ago."

And she sighed. The mayor had a troubling thought.

"Don't tell me you're pregnant too!"

"What do you mean, me too? What does that mean?"

"Nothing. Are or aren't you?"

"No, I'm not! What's got into you?"

The mayor didn't answer. He just lay down, and five minutes later was already snoring. Signura Filippa stayed up a long time, sighing in frustration.

Chapter V
The Consequences of the Cholera and Other Matters

Dr. Enrico Palumbo was, in a sense, the poor people's doctor, just as the lawyer was their defender. The difference between the two was that the doctor didn't do what he did for any political ideal, but just because he wanted to.

Oftentimes, after examining some sick child from a penniless family, he would leave the mother as much money as she needed to buy medicine or cook up a dish of pasta. He hated priests perhaps even more than Teresi did. The only man of the cloth in town he respected was Patre Dalli Cardillo.

And the doctor was a man with guts. He never said a word to anyone about any of the things he came to know.

At dawn on the day after the cholera brouhaha he went knocking on Teresi's door. The lawyer answered the door himself.

"Did he make it through the night all right?" he immediately asked.

"He was delirious."

"Fever?"

"A hundred and four."

"Let's go and see him."

As he was climbing the stairs, the doctor asked:

"How about your nephew?"

"He's gone to bed. We took turns."

They'd put the injured young man in a small room barely big enough to fit a single bed, a chair, and a bedside table.

"Would you like some coffee?"

"Yes, thanks."

Teresi went into the kitchen, made the coffee, and then brought it to him. The doctor took a sip.

"What do you think?"

"About the coffee?"

"No, about the kid."

"I haven't had a good look at him yet. But the main thing is that he made it through the night."

The doctor handed the little cup back to Teresi.

"I'll be waiting in my study," said Teresi. "Call me if you need anything."

He sat down and started thinking about the things he'd heard coming from the delirious young man's mouth during the night. Not that he really understood any of it; all that came out were truncated words mumbled by a mouth missing three teeth, through swollen lips as big as cucumbers.

" . . . no . . . no . . . pleeathe . . . no more . . . no . . . no . . . "

This part, unfortunately, was all too comprehensible.

" . . . on flefo . . . pleeathe . . . on flefo . . . "

He'd also said other things Teresi couldn't understand. *Flefo. Flefo.*

Maybe he was saying *no flefo*. What did it mean? Nothing. How about *Don't flay me*? No, that didn't really fit. Perhaps *Don thay tho*—that is, *Don't say so*? But maybe the *. . . on* didn't mean "don't" at all. Wait a second. Maybe it was a mangled way of saying *I'm not afraid of you*: *. . . no' fray 'f'ou*. No, that didn't work either. If the lad wasn't afraid, then why would he plead for the person to stop?

Wait. What if it was *Don Flefo*?

The doctor came in.

"Do you know anyone by the name of Don Flefo?"

"No. What an odd name. Listen, do you know how to give someone a shot?"

"Yes."

"Then give him this in four hours. I'll leave you the syringe and the medicine. I don't want to come here too often, otherwise people might notice."

"How did you find him?"

"Better. He's a strong, healthy young man. He'll definitely recover. I'll be back to give him a third shot this evening, around nine."

After the doctor left, Teresi started thinking again about what the lad had said during the night.

Let's put aside this *flefo* for a minute. What did he say after that?

. . . no . . . no . . . tu ariddru . . . ttu ariddru. . . no . . . cent . . . gno . . . no . . . cent . . . gno . . .

The lawyer stopped at this point, leaving aside the other things he'd heard the boy say. He grabbed a sheet of paper and a pencil. Best go about this in orderly fashion. He was going to work something out of this muddle, even if it took him all day. And he was convinced that whatever it was, it would allow him to screw don Filadelfo Cammarata, the marquis.

Wait a second, Matté, he said to himself.

Don Filadelfo. *Don Flefo*. That could be it. *Don Flefo* might very well be don Filadelfo.

*

At eight o'clock the following morning, as the mayor was going up to his office in City Hall, the usher warned him:

"The captain's here, you know."

What a constant pain in the arse that man was! With some effort, the mayor managed to smile as he entered his office.

"My good captain!"

"Good morning," the other said drily.

He was sitting in the armchair in front of the desk. The mayor took possession of his own chair.

"A quiet night?" he asked.

"Quiet as can be," Montagnet replied. Then he said: "Did you summon Don Raccuglia?"

"I'll do so immediately."

"There's no longer any need."

Mayor Calandro felt a little relieved. The fewer priests around, the better for all involved.

"Well, I'm gla—"

"I changed my mind," the captain continued. "I went and paid him a call at church."

"When?"

"At six o'clock this morning. I waited for him to finish saying the first Mass, which was a mass of thanksgiving for the passing of the cholera menace. The church was packed."

Well, thanks a lot, captain dickhead! Might as well have gone there with a brass band and woken up the whole town! First he says he wants no speculation or malicious gossip and then he goes and shows up in uniform in front of all of Don Raccuglia's parishoners!

"Did you speak to him?"

"Of course. In the sacristy."

"And what did you say to him?"

"That I'd denounced him to the court of Camporeale for sedition and inciting public disorder."

Well at least he didn't put him up in front of a firing squad! But did this captain see things backwards or something?

"But, Captain, that's not exactly the way things went."

"Oh, no? Then how, exactly, did things go?"

So now the man was going to play the wise guy?

"If there's anyone in town inciting people to rebel, it's the lawyer Teresi! You have no idea what the man says and writes!"

"You're wrong, I do have an idea. His weekly comes to Camporeale, and I read it. As part of my duty, of course."

"So you know perfectly well which of the two men is the real subversive. It's Teresi!"

"Allow me please to firmly disagree. In this specific case, it wasn't the lawyer leading the unrest, but the priest."

"But you must try to understand Don Raccuglia! Teresi advances ideas which—"

"—Which in no way authorize Don Raccuglia to stir up the population against him."

"But he dared fire a gun at the crucifix!"

"He fired in self-defense. If I take any action against him, I must also take action against don Liborio Spartà and his wife, and against the Veronica brothers. What do you think about that?"

Clever man, this captain. The mayor weighed his options.

"I think you're right."

"Thank you. And as for the fact that he shot at the crucifix, I would advise you not to insist too much on that version of events. First, because the lawyer shot in the air. And second, because, even if he had fired at the crowd, he would have been firing at a priest using the crucifix to break down his door."

The mayor said nothing. But the captain didn't let up.

"And now, would you please give me the name of the person who sowed the rumor about the cholera?"

Mayor Calandro had given this a lot of thought after his long discussion with Dr. Bellanca.

"All right," he said. "I checked into the matter and came up with the name of a very stable person considered by all to be a serious man of great integrity. And not only, but—"

"Are you talking about don Anselmo Buttafava?" asked the captain, interrupting him.

Calandro's eyes opened wide.

"But how . . . how did you know that?"

"We're carabinieri, my good man. At five o'clock this morning I sent five of my men out to arrest him."

"But do you know where he is?"

"Of course. I've learned that Signor Buttafava owns an estate called San Giusippuzzo. And he also manages another, La Forcaiola, for a cousin of his who's presently in jail. He's either at San Giusippuzzo or La Forcaiola, there's no two ways about it. I think he'll be back here in town by eleven at the latest."

Don Anselmo, arrested by the carabinieri? Was this asshole trying to trigger a revolution or something?

"In . . . handcuffs?"

"No. There's no reason for that. Don't worry, he'll be treated with the utmost consideration. Along with the two carabinieri I also sent Lieutenant Villasevaglios."

"Speaking of consideration . . . "

"Tell me."

"The municipal physician, Dr. Bellanca, told me last night that he can explain how don Anselmo came to misconstrue the situation. May I have him come?"

"Of course," said the captain, rising to his feet. "And now, if you'll allow me, I have to leave you. I have a few little things to attend to. I'm going to ring His Excellency the Prefect by telephone to set his mind at rest. And while I'm at it, I'm going to ring His Excellency the Bishop as well."

Was this man insane? The bishop? So now he was going to go and bust the bishop's chops as well? Why? A bout of genuine cholera might really have been less of a plague than this goddamn captain!

"I'm sorry, but why the bishop?"

"Well, you know, it may not be in my line of duty, but I think it's only common courtesy to inform him that I have reported one of his priests. I'll see you back here at eleven."

I hope you break your neck, the mayor said to him in his mind.

*

His Excellency the Most Reverend Monsignor Egilberto Martire put down the telephone receiver and grabbed a notepad he had on the table. He opened it, thumbed through it, tore out a sheet, and then rang the little bell he kept within reach.

"You rang, Your Excellency?" said his secretary, Don Marcantonio Panza.

"Don Marcantonio, on this sheet of paper are the names of the priests of the eight parishes in Palizzolo. I haven't yet made my episcopal visits, so I don't know them yet. I want them all here, at the bishopric, at four o'clock this afternoon. I will not tolerate any absences."

"Yes, sir."

Working with His Excellency Egilberto Martire was worse than living in a barracks. Physically, he looked more like a sergeant major than a bishop. Fat, short, and with a red face that, when he got upset, started to turn purple. In the six months since he arrived at Camporeale, he'd instituted a military-style discipline. The best of it was that, being Roman, every so often he would speak in obscenities.

"The stupid shits!" Don Marcantonio heard him in fact say as he was leaving the room.

*

Don Anselmo Buttafava did not come in at eleven o'clock, for the simple reason that before reaching La Forcaiola, Lieutenant Villasevaglios and the two carabinieri ran into some trouble. And therefore don Anselmo didn't find out that day that he was supposed to report to Captain Montagnet to defend himself against the accusation of disturbing the peace. Right where the trail to La Forcaiola branched off into a smaller trail leading into the Galluzzo district, there stood a giant olive tree. Up in the boughs of this tree a brigand from the Salamone gang was hiding, a man known as *Savaturi 'u pecuru*—"Salvatore the Sheep"—because the great quantity of hair he had all over his body. He was standing guard. Seeing the three soldiers approach, he gave a shepherd's whistle to sound the alarm.

Salamone the brigand, who the night before had seized three women fleeing from Palizzolo, was having his way with them inside a nearby cave. Outside the cave, keeping watch, were two trusted brigands, Arelio the Hare and Pancrazio the Snake.

The rest of the gang had headed on towards the Arbanazzo woods a few miles away.

Hearing the whistle, Arelio and Pancrazio ran over to the olive tree and took up position. As soon as the carabinieri were within range, they started shooting. The three soldiers dismounted, took cover behind some trees, and returned fire. After five minutes of firing back and forth, the lieutenant signaled to the two carabinieri and, slithering along the ground through the grass, he came close to the tree from which Savaturi *'u pecuru* was firing, took careful aim, and cut him down with one shot.

Savaturi's dead body fell right onto Pancrazio's head, whereupon the bandit shot to his feet only to fall back down again a second later, struck by another bullet from the lieutenant, who was a peerless marksman. Scared to death, Arelio the Hare started running towards the cave, yelling. The carabinieri gave chase, and two things happened at once. As Arelio fell down, dead, at the mouth of the grotto, out of the same grotto came Salamone the brigand, naked and a little woozy from having repeatedly ravished the three women. As soon as he saw the three carabinieri, he realized he was done for and put his hands up. Behind him, in tears, appeared the three women, also naked, who ran into the carabinieri's arms saying they'd been sent by God to deliver them from a certain death at the hands of the bandits. After giving the women a chance to put their clothes back on, the lieutenant let them go as they wished. That way they could tell everyone that Salamone had treated them like queens and respected them like Madonnas.

The only person Lieutenant Villasevaglios had to escort back to Palizzolo was therefore Salamone, and he forced the brigand to trudge into town in his underpants, which he'd been allowed to put back on so as not to offend common decency and bound in ropes so tight he looked like a walking salami being pulled along by a horse.

Less than an hour after reaching Palizzolo, Salamone was "made to pay the consequences" by order of Captain Montagnet. The corpses of the other three brigands were hung from nearby trees.

This time there were a lot of people attending the execution in front of the wall of the ancient convent.

*

The clock was striking the twelve chimes of midday when Stefano woke up. *Matre santa!* He'd fallen asleep instead of taking over for his uncle!

He got dressed in a hurry and went into the young man's room. His uncle wasn't there, but the injured youth was sleeping and didn't seem agitated. Stefano placed his palm on the sleeper's forehead: the fever seemed to have dropped a little.

He went downstairs and into his uncle's study. Teresi was sleeping, mouth open, head leaning against the back of the armchair. On the table he noticed some sheets of paper with writing on them. As he turned to leave, to let his uncle sleep, Teresi opened his eyes and called to him.

"Stefano, come here!"

The tone of his voice sounded pleased.

"Sit down."

And he handed him a sheet of paper.

. . . no . . . no . . . pleeathe . . . no more . . . no . . . no . . . on flefo . . . pleeathe . . . on flefo . . . no . . . no . . . tu ariddru . . . no . . . cent . . . I . . . no . . . cent . . . no . . . cent . . . . . . ahhh . . . ahhh . . . ndu . . . nuthin . . . olina . . . oww . . . no . . . no . . . nuthin . . . o . . . olina . . .

"So? That's the stuff the guy was saying last night, all strung together. But it doesn't make any sense."

Teresi chuckled.

"Did you manage to make some sense of it?" Stefano asked.

"In fact I think I did," said his uncle.

He handed him another sheet of paper.

. . . no . . . no . . . please . . . no more . . . no . . . no . . . don Filadelfo . . . please . . . don Filadelfo . . . no . . . no . . . 'zù Carmineddru . . . I'm innocent . . . I'm innocent . . . innocent . . . ahhh . . . ahhh . . . I didn't do nothing to Paolina . . . ahhh . . . no . . . no . . . nothing to Paolina . . .

Stefano turned pale. Then Teresi slapped himself hard on the forehead.

"The shot!"

He grabbed the medicine and syringe and raced down the stairs.

"Except for that one . . . what's your name?" Bishop Egilberto Martire asked the oldest of the eight priests lined up in front of him.

"Mariano Dalli Cardillo, Your Excellency."

"How old are you?"

"Seventy."

"Now, going from right to left, the names and ages of everyone else."

"Alessio Terranova, forty-three years old."

"Eriberto Raccuglia, forty years old."

"Filiberto Cusa, forty-one years old."

"Libertino Samonà, forty-five years old"

"Angelo Marrafà, forty years old."

"Ernesto Pintacuda, thirty-nine years old."

"So, with the exception of Don Dalli Cardillo, the rest of you are young. Too young to understand in full the responsibilities that rest on the shoulders of a parish priest—and not just religious responsibilities. This was a grave mistake my predecessor made. He should have taken care to ensure that it didn't happen. I will try to set things right as quickly as possible. But let's get to the point. This morning I was told by Carabinieri Captain Montagnet, who was sent to Palizzolo over that cholera idiocy, that you, Don Raccuglia, were so goddamn stupid as to get yourself reported for sedition. Nice going! A seditious priest!"

"I'd like to explain, Your Excellency . . . " Don Raccuglia began.

"You're not going to explain anything to me, got that?"

"But . . . "

"Shut up! Here you talk only when I say so! And that's not all! The good captain also informed me that in all the churches, except for that of Don Dalli Cardillo, you incited the faithful, from your pulpits, against Teresi the lawyer! You incited the faithful to hatred! Come on! Where are you, anyway! You're in Church, for Christ's sake! In church you're supposed to preach love, and only love should spread outward from the church! Have you forgotten what Jesus said? Love thy neighbor as thyself! That's what Jesus said! You say: But Teresi the lawyer wants to destroy the family! So what! And you, instead of preaching love for the family and the sanctity of matrimony, you start preaching against some lawyer? Are you shitting me? Fight that lawyer with your own weapons, not with his! Take one Sunday, any Sunday, when the sun is shining bright, and declare it Family Day! Have all the married couples with all their children come to the church. Then organize a big feast in the churchyard! With singing and dancing! And everyone will smile and laugh and say: What a great thing the family is! What a beautiful thing is the sacrament of holy matrimony! And then you all eat and drink your fill to spite Teresi the lawyer! Do we understand one another now?"

"There is no other explanation, Stefanù, believe me."

"But that's not possible, Zio! So, in your opinion, Paolina, the Marquis Cammarata's eldest daughter, is also pregnant, like Antonietta?"

"That's exactly right."

"And don Filadelfo, thinking that his daughter's lover was that relative of his wife, and knowing that the kid was coming to see them, sent for *'u zù* Carmineddru and had him beat him within an inch of his life?"

"That's exactly right."

"I don't believe it."

"Do you have any other way to explain what happened?"

"Well, it's exactly like what happened to me, except that the baron wanted to shoot me."

"I agree with you there."

"So what do we do now?"

"For the moment, nothing. If the kid confirms what I've been thinking—and let's hope he recovers soon—then I'll see to finishing off the marquis myself!"

One of the three women that Salamone the brigand had enjoyed in the grotto was a pretty, firm-fleshed girl by the name of Rosalia Pampina. The orphaned daughter of a peasant couple, she worked as a maid at the home of Giallonardo the notary. Since the notary was a parishioner of Don Filiberto Cusa's church, the girl had obtained permission to attend her employer's church, the church of San Cono.

On the afternoon of the same day she was freed by the

carabinieri, she went back to work at the notary's house. But she said nothing to him about what the brigand had done to her. She merely told him she'd run off to the country to flee from the threat of cholera. At vespers, however, she asked Signura Romilda Giallonardo for permission to go to church to thank the Lord for delivering her from danger. Rosalia was a very devout girl and an avid churchgoer, so much so that Signura Romilda often told her she should become a nun.

She would recite all the decades of the rosary upon awaking each morning and in the evening when she went to bed, and she never missed the day's first Mass. Oftentimes Patre Cusa, who had noticed her great religious devotion, would call her into the sacristy to explain the catechism to her. For this reason Signura Romilda saw no reason not to allow her to go out now.

"I would like to confess," Rosalia said to Don Filiberto, calling him aside as he was closing the great door of the church.

"It's late now. Come back tomorrow morning."

"No, sir. You need to hear my confession right away."

The priest looked at her and saw that she was crying.

"All right," he said, leading her to the confessional.

He sat down inside, made the sign of the cross, put on his stole, said a prayer, and opened the little door over the grate.

"What happened to you, my child?"

"I lost my virginity."

And she started weeping audibly. Luckily there was nobody else in the church.

"How did that happen? So first you go out and have a good time, then you come in hear and start crying, you wretch?" the priest said in indignation.

"No, no! I didn't have a good time at all! Salamone the brigand did it to me!"

And she started telling him what had happened to her. The

priest, as was his duty, interrupted her every so often, asking her for more details.

"Twice from the front and twice from behind?! The horror! The horror!"

"So he really hurt you?"

"And you, did you enjoy it when he was . . . "

In the end, Rosalia started shouting.

"My soul is damned! Damned for eternity! Even though you had me drink holy water to protect me, I've damned myself just the same!"

"No, Rosalia, don't say that. The holy water springing from my body was to protect you from yourself, from the temptations you might have. But this is another matter! You were forced. You did not do it of your own free will! You are not to blame!"

"Is that really true?"

"Yes, it's true. Your soul is unblemished, but your body has been gravely contaminated. Sullied. We must make it pure and clean again."

"But how, Father?"

"Through the penance I will have you do."

Chapter VI
Things Get Complicated

Four days after the famous day of cholera, at eight o'clock in the morning, don Anselmo Buttafava and his wife got in their carriage to head back to Palizzolo from La Forcaiola. Lieutenant Villasevaglios, who would escort them back to town along with the two mounted carabinieri, had managed to convince him that there had never been any cholera. He also told him that Captain Montagnet wanted urgently to talk to him, but despite all of don Anselmo's questions, he never explained why.

Since to return to Palizzolo they had no choice but to pass by San Giusippuzzo, don Anselmo was granted permission to stop at his villa for a moment to fetch a pair of eyeglasses he'd left there the night they'd fled to La Forcaiola. When he entered the compound, he noticed that the front door of farm overseer 'Ngilino's house was closed, as were all the shutters on the windows. 'Ngilino must surely have been making the rounds of the estate, but how could Catarina and Totina still be sick? Don Anselmo went into the villa, retrieved his glasses, and just as he was climbing back into the carriage, saw a wisp of smoke rising from the overseer's house. So there was indeed someone inside!

"Just one minute," he said to the lieutenant.

And he went and knocked on the overseer's door. Catarina, who'd been watching him from behind the shutters, remained absolutely silent and didn't move.

"Ma, you can't not open the door for him," said Totina, who was standing beside her.

"Why?"

"Because he's with the carabinieri."

Catarina came downstairs and opened the door.

"Good morning, sir."

"Good morning, Catarì. Why wouldn't you open the door?"

"I have the flu, sir, and had to get out of bed."

"What about Totina?"

"She's also in bed."

"I'll go and comfort her," said don Anselmo, putting his handkerchief over his face to avoid catching germs and advancing towards the entrance.

Catarina blocked his path.

"No, sir, you can't come in!"

Don Anselmo got incensed. How dare this peasant woman talk to him like that? He shoved her aside and went in. Totina was standing next to the window in her bedroom.

There are women who can be pregnant even up to eight months without anyone noticing, and there are others who already at two months have a belly so big that they look like they might give birth at any moment. Totina belonged to the latter category.

Don Anselmo, having entered on the run, froze in his tracks. Behind him he heard Catarina weeping. Then he took two steps forward and dealt the girl a hard slap in the face. But she didn't budge, didn't raise her arm to protect herself, and only stood there, immobile, staring at him.

"Who was it?"

She didn't answer.

"Who was it?" he repeated, raising his hand again.

"It was the Holy Spirit."

So the slut wanted to joke around, did she? Don Anselmo could barely restrain the urge to start kicking her in the belly.

"Strumpet!"

Then, to Catarina:

"Tomorrow morning I want to see 'Ngilino!"

He turned his back, went down the stairs, and got back in the carriage.

*

"Where am I?

These were the first words that came out of the young man's mouth as he opened his eyes and saw someone he thought he recognized sitting in the chair beside the bed.

"At the home of friends."

"How long have I been sick?"

Sick? Didn't he remember any of what had happened to him?

"Just a minute," said Stefano. Then he called loudly: "Zio, come upstairs! The kid is awake!"

Teresi climbed the stairs two at a time.

"How long have I been sick?" the lad asked the new arrival.

"A few days," Teresi answered vaguely.

"Has my mother been informed?"

"Young man," said the lawyer, "we found you in the street."

He decided it was best to spare the lad the detail about the sack. And he continued:

"And we didn't find anything in your pockets: no papers, no money. So how could we have informed your mother?"

"My name is Luigino Chiarapane, and I live in Salsetto, in the palazzo next to town hall."

"I'll get on it at once," said Teresi.

"But what happened to me?"

"I really don't know," said Teresi. "But don't strain yourself trying to remember. You've talked enough. For now you should just go back to sleep."

They shut his window and went down to the study.

"I'll go and get the horse. I'll be back in an hour," said Stefano.

"Where are you going?"

"To Salsetto, what do you think?"

"To do what?"

"What do you mean, 'to do what'? To go and tell his mother . . . "

"You're not going to tell anyone."

"But, Zio, the poor woman must be worried to death!"

"Stefanù, until the kid begins to remember everything, nobody must know he's here! I smell something fishy in this whole affair. Something very fishy. This is a card to play against the marquis, and I don't want to waste it!"

"Could someone please tell me why I've been summoned here?" don Anselmo asked at once, still in a rage from the sight of the pregnant Totina.

They were in Mayor Calandro's office in City Hall. The captain had taken an armchair for himself and placed it next to the mayor's. Don Anselmo was sitting opposite them, across the desk.

"I can tell you straightaway," said Montagnet. "Everyone I questioned named you as the person who first spread the false information that there was a cholera outbreak in town. It is my duty to ascertain whether you did so intentionally or by mistake. That's all."

"The only person I told was my wife. And in private. In our home. As you see, I didn't spread a goddamn thing!"

The mayor squirmed in his chair. From the morning sky you can tell what kind of day it's going to be, and in this case the sky was already full of dark storm clouds.

"I beg you please to temper your language," the captain said frostily.

"May I explain what actually happened, so we can clear things up and stop wasting my time?" said don Anselmo.

"Do you think this is a waste of your time?" asked Montagnet.

"I don't *think* it's a waste of my time, it *is* a waste of my time."

Without saying a word, the captain got up and headed for the door.

"Where are you going?" asked the mayor in alarm. This guy was liable to have even don Anselmo put up against the wall to "pay the consequences."

"I'm going to call the lieutenant and turn him over."

"Turn me over?" said don Anselmo, springing to his feet. "And how would like me cooked? Rare? Well done?"

The mayor ran over to the captain and practically knelt down in front of him.

"Oh, please, for God's sake, don't do that! I will take it upon myself personally, as mayor, to vouch for don Anselmo Buttafava's good behavior! And you, don Anselmo, what are you doing? Trying to ruin us all?"

"I apologize," said don Anselmo.

They all sat back down.

"Please tell me your version of events," Montagnet said to don Anselmo. "But I'm warning you: if I'm not convinced by what you say, I will arrest you for willful disturbance of the public order!"

Don Anselmo turned red in the face and opened his mouth to answer in kind, but a powerful kick from the mayor under the table persuaded him to sit tight.

"Go on, speak," the captain urged him.

Don Anselmo, who on his way to City Hall had stopped at home to change his clothes and learned the maid Giseffa's side of the story, told the captain how he'd become convinced that there was cholera about and had said so to his wife, who then repeated it to their aged housekeeper Suntina, who then confided this news to the young maid, Giseffa. The girl had then run home to her father's house and spilled the beans, the rumor began to spread, and, in the end, all hell broke loose.

"There's still one point that needs to be cleared up," said the captain. "Which is: What made you think there was an outbreak of cholera?"

With saintly patience, don Anselmo explained how it had been Dr. Bellanca who had first raised his suspicions. Seeing the doctor running between Palazzo Lo Mascolo and Palazzo Cammarata, he'd asked him what was going on, and Bellanca had replied in such a way that he could only conclude . . .

"All right," the captain said when don Anselmo had finished, "you're dismissed."

Don Anselmo stood up, held out his hand to the mayor, and Montagnet suddenly tensed up.

"You're not free to go yet, you know," he said icily. "I merely meant you're dismissed to go and wait in the room next door."

"Of all the goddamn . . . " don Ansemo began.

But the mayor put a hand over his mouth and pushed him into the next room. The captain hadn't noticed anything, because he'd stood up and gone out of the office. He returned a moment later with Dr. Bellanca, sat him down in don Anselmo's place, and said:

"Doctor, Signor Buttafava just now told us that you were the cause of his misunderstanding, because when he saw you making house calls at both Palazzo Lo Mascolo and Palazzo Cammarata, you told him that the baron and his entire family, as well as the marquis and his entire family, were sick, but you didn't specify what the illness was. Is this correct?"

"Yes, I confirm in full."

"It seems to me that at this point there's no further need . . . " said the mayor.

But the captain seemed not to have heard him.

"Why didn't you explicitly tell Signor Buttafava that it was a simple case of influenza, however serious? If you had, Signor Buttafava would not have misconstrued the situation."

"Well, he was irritating me with his insistent curiosity. And anyway, professional ethics don't—"

"I see. So was it really a grave form of flu?"

"Of course!"

"Do you remember what Marquis Cammarata's temperature was on Sunday morning?"

"Not really . . . but it was at least 101 or 102 . . . "

"So then why did the marquis go to the club that morning?"

"He's a stubborn man, you know. They were voting on whether to admit the lawyer Teresi for membership . . . I'd told him not to get out of bed, but . . . In fact, when he got back home, his condition worsened."

"Whereas Baron Lo Mascolo took your advice and stayed in bed."

What the hell was the guy getting at? the mayor wondered. Luckily, however, Dr. Bellanca didn't crack.

"He couldn't have even if he'd wanted to. He was the sickest of them all!"

"He had a high fever?"

"Very high. A hundred and four."

"On Monday morning too?"

The question caught the doctor by surprise.

"I . . . really don't know . . . I don't remember . . . "

"Please try to remember."

"Let me think . . . Monday morning, you say? Well, if it wasn't a hundred and four, it was around a hundred and three, I'd say."

"And how do you explain that around seven o'clock on Monday morning, or shortly thereafter, he was stopped by one of Marshal Sciabarrà's carabinieri on the walkway behind Teresi's residence?"

Bellanca looked at him with his mouth agape. The mayor turned pale.

"They . . . arrested him?"

"No. When the marshal learned that a number of ruffians being led by a priest were laying siege to the lawyer's house, he sent two of his men. One of them saw a peasant having some trouble descending a narrow alley, and so he followed him and then stopped him. But then he recognized the baron and let him go."

"I'm sorry, but why did you say the carabiniere had seen a peasant?"

"Because the baron was disguised as a peasant."

Now the mayor's jaw dropped in surprise. He no longer understood anything. What on earth was happening in that accursèd town?

"And what did the baron say to the carabiniere?" asked the doctor.

"He said he'd gone out for a breath of air."

"And why was he disguised?"

"He didn't want to be bothered by any acquaintances during his walk."

"Maybe he'd gone to see Teresi."

"That's his business," the captain said by way of conclusion. "But the upshot of all this, doctor, is that you're clearly lying. I'll give you five minutes' time to make up your mind; if, by then, you haven't told me the truth, I will have you arrested."

And so it was that, as don Anselmo was on his way home, cursing out loud like a madman, Dr. Bellanca emerged from City Hall in handcuffs, flanked by two carabinieri.

The captain had charged and released on bail don Anselmo, and imprisoned the doctor, for "working together on a criminal project the purpose of which is not yet clear." They had "created a grave public disturbance, artfully spreading alarming rumors designed to sow panic among the local population."

As news of Dr. Bellanca's arrest and the charges against don Anselmo began to spread, a number of things happened.

Don Liborio Spartà sent the club's manservant Casimiro from house to house to summon the executive committee for a meeting to be held at five o'clock that afternoon. But the committee members had to come one at a time, without attracting any attention, since martial law was in effect.

Mayor Calandro, for his part, got on the phone to talk to the prefect. He told His Excellency, Commendator Eustachio Benincasa, that the town had been left without a municipal doctor after the—in his opinion—arbitrary arrest of the holder of that title, and it therefore behooved His Excellency to appoint a physician from the provincial capital and send him to Palizzolo. He also told him that seeing Dr. Bellanca, a man loved and esteemed by all, walk down the street in handcuffs had been a terrible blow for the whole town. In short, His Excellency should be aware that there was general resentment over Captain Montagnet's way of going about things.

He'd just set the phone down when, without bothering to knock, don Serafino Labianca, Commendator Agusto Paladino, and Patre Alighiero Scurria, the parish priest of the Heart of Jesus church, walked in.

"Is it true . . . "

" . . . that the captain . . . "

" . . . arrested the doctor?"

This was the first tripartite question asked.

"Yes, it's true."

"Is it true . . .

" . . . that don Anselmo . . . "

" . . . has been charged and released on his own recognizance?"

This was the second tripartite question.

"Yes, it's true."

"That captain is a maniac!" said Patre Scurria.

"And why did he arrest Bellanca?" asked don Serafino.

"Because the doctor didn't want to tell him what the marquis and the baron were sick with. Or, more precisely, he told them they had the flu, but Montagnet didn't believe him."

"Sheer lunacy!" said Patre Scurria. "But doesn't the good captain know that a doctor is like a priest? We can't just tell others what we're told in the confessional, and doctors are not free to tell other what their patients are sick with."

"This is a clear abuse of power!" don Serafino exclaimed.

"It's a classic example of the Piedmontese disdain for us Sicilians," the commendatore proclaimed. "But I'm not going to let this asshole off easy. I'm going to my office now to call Ciccino Barrafranca in Rome and tell him the whole story, and ask him to take immediate action."

The honorable parliamentary deputy Francesco Barrafranca, a first cousin and very good friend of the commendatore's, had owed his resounding electoral victory in Palizzolo to none other than Commendatore Agusto Paladino.

"And I," said the mayor, "have just finished speaking with the prefect. I told him there was a lot of resentment building up around town."

"And this state of martial law certainly can't last until the next cholera outbreak," said don Serafino. "It must be lifted at once, no later than tomorrow."

At seven o'clock that evening, the executive committee of the Honor and Family Social Club, consisting of don Liborio Spartà, don Stapino Vassallo, Colonel Amasio Petrosillo, and

Professor Ubaldo Malatesta, finished drafting a petition to the prefect of the provincial capital, Camporeale, in which they claimed that the entire population of Palizzolo was indignant over the charges brought by Captain Montagnet against three individuals so beloved and venerated as don Anselmo Buttafava, Don Raccuglia, and Dr. Bellanca, the latter having even been unjustly incarcerated. The town's citizens therefore demanded:

—that all charges against said persons be dropped;

—that Dr. Bellanca be freed at once;

—that the declaration of martial law be revoked, as there was no longer any reason for it.

The club's manservant, Casimiro, was assigned the task of collecting the signatures of not only the club's members, but also anyone else who wished to add his or her name.

That evening, Dr. Girlanno Presti arrived from Camporeale to fill in for the municipal doctor. The first thing Presti did was to introduce himself to Captain Montagnet, telling him he needed to confer with Dr. Bellanca in order to have a better sense of the health conditions of the townfolk. Montagnet granted him permission to talk to the doctor at eight o'clock the following morning.

*

"So, now that I've told where and how we found you, and I've explained to you why I thought it would be better if I brought you back to my house instead of to Palazzo Cammarata, are you ready to tell us everything?"

"Yes," said Luigi Chiarapane.

The lad had recovered fairly well, the compresses had reduced the swelling in his lips, his fever was now under 100, but his three broken ribs still hurt whenever he made the slightest movement.

"I want to see them both in jail: the marquis and *'u zù* Carmineddru," said Luigino, almost as if to himself.

"I do too," Teresi smiled. "So please tell me everything from the very beginning."

"My mother is a cousin of Filadelfo Cammarata's wife, and while we were still living in Palizzolo—up until I turned fifteen—our families spent a lot of time together. I grew up with Paolina, the marquis's eldest daughter, though I'm three years older than her. Even after we moved to Salsetto, I've always kept coming back here, at least twice a week, to see her. I'm an only child, and Paolina for me was the sister I never had. She's a jewel of a girl—religious, good-hearted and unselfish. I have no idea how she got into this situation!"

"We'll talk about that later," said Teresi.

"The other day when there was all the cholera confusion, my mother herself told me to come to Palizzolo to see how the Cammaratas were doing. First she'd sent a servant to ask the marquis if I could drop by his house in the afternoon, and he'd answered yes. I started to get worried as soon as I saw the front door closed and the windows shuttered. It looked like they were in mourning, so I was afraid somebody had died. I knocked on the door and Gnazina, their eleven-year-old daughter, came and told me that all the servants had run away and Paolina and everybody else in the house were sick with the flu. Then she took me into the marquis's study and told me to wait there. The house was as quiet as a graveyard, when normally it's a pretty noisy place. About a half an hour later, the marquis came in. He was angry and more nervous than usual. He told me to come with him down to the cellar for a minute to fetch a bottle of wine, and so I followed behind him.

"'How is Paolina?' I asked.

"He didn't answer, but just opened the cellar door. It was already lit up in there, with oil lamps.

"'I have to do something first,' he said. 'You go on downstairs, I'll be along in a minute.'

"As soon as I got to the bottom of the stone staircase, which is quite long, I heard the door close. I thought it was a gust of wind. Then suddenly, standing before me was *'u zù* Carmineddru."

"Did you already know him?" Teresi asked.

"Yes. He would come and call on the marquis, and they would shut themselves up in his study."

"Did you know who he was?"

"How could I not know? Everybody in town knows he's a man of influence."

"And what did he say to you?"

"Say to me? He didn't say a word."

"What did he do?"

"He laid me out on the floor with his first punch in the face. Then it was all kicks and blows with a kind of club . . . I was yelling and screaming, but who's gonna hear me there in the cellar? After he'd been beating me for about ten minutes, don Filadelfo came in. 'So you had a good time with my daughter Paolina, eh, you pig? Got her pregnant, eh, you dog? Well, you're a dead man now.' I swear before God that this news hurt me more than any of the things *zù* Carmineddru was doing to me. At that point they both started pummeling me. And then I fainted and don't remember anything else."

"They thought you were dead," said Stefano.

"And we're going to let them keep thinking you're dead," said Teresi.

Chapter VII
The Day of Denunciation

Girlanno Presti was a good doctor, but in Camporeale he was known as someone who was afraid of his own shadow.

He lived with a man who was actually more of a walking tree trunk than a man. His name was Costantino, and he was so big and so broad that he was frightening just to look at. He was always at the doctor's disposal, ready to accompany him out on nighttime house calls, since never in a million years would the doctor have gone out into the darkness alone.

He would get scared out of his wits at the slightest thing, and already the mere fact of having to go to the carabinieri station at eight o'clock in the morning had made him break out in a cold sweat. But what surprised him most was that he found his colleague, Dr. Bellanca, as fresh and calm as if he'd just spent the night at the Grand Hotel. Bellanca knew Presti and was relieved they'd chosen him to replace him. Montagnet had set no time limit on the meeting between the two doctors and had made a room with a table and two chairs available to them. The first thing Bellanca said was:

"Did you bring a lot of changes of clothes?"

"No. Why do you ask?"

"Because I don't think they'll free me any time soon. Yesterday evening the captain came and told me that I could be in here till the end of my days if I didn't start talking. And I won't talk. So . . . "

"But what does he want to know?"

"He wants to know what Baron Lo Mascolo and Marquis Camarata are sick with. I told him the flu, but he won't believe it."

"So what are they sick with?"

"They're not sick at all. But I can hardly throw mud on the honorable names of two families!"

Girlanno Presti turned pale. What was this new complication? He knew his colleague was charged with disturbing the peace, and now it's a question of the honor of two families? The word *honor*, in Sicily, was a dangerous matter, one that almost always led to bloodshed.

"Is this something I should know?" he asked, secretly hoping Bellanca would say no.

"Of course! Are you not fulfilling the function of town doctor now?"

Bellanca told him everything.

"Four pregnant women, none of whom is married? And all of them two months pregnant? How do you explain that?" Presti asked in bewilderment.

"There is no explanation. That's the problem. And I'll have you know that these four pregnancies already raise the annual average in Palizzolo. They're a surplus, a bonus. A flowering out of season. Know what I mean? But not a word about this to anyone, do you hear?"

Presti looked offended.

"No need to remind me of that."

"And now let's discuss the town's health situation. Around here, tracoma and malaria . . . "

They talked for about an hour, after which they shook hands and a carabiniere came to take Dr. Bellanca away. As Presti was gathering up the papers on which he'd been taking notes, the door opened again.

He looked up to see Montagnet staring at him like a cat eyeing a mouse.

*

Dr. Palumbo, for his part, arrived late for his morning visit to Teresi's house. He found the young man quite improved, and told him that in three days or so he would be able to get out of bed and walk around the house a little.

"But Teresi's nephew told my mother I was here, and she'll be coming to see me this afternoon. She wants to take me back to Salsetto."

"For the moment that's out of the question. You're not strong enough to handle a journey in a carriage."

After the examination, Teresi offered the doctor a cup of coffee.

"Sorry I got here late, but I was called to Giallonardo's house."

"Is the notary sick?"

"No, he's fine, as is his wife."

"So what was the problem? They haven't got any children!"

"It's the maid. A pretty twenty-five-year-old by the name of Rosalia Pampina—or, so Signura Giallonardo told me, since the girl has stopped talking."

"What do you mean, she's stopped talking?"

"The girl ran away when she heard about the cholera. She spent one day and one night away, then came back the following afternoon. Ever since, she's stopped talking, eating, and drinking. Or, rather, when she got back she asked her mistress if she could go to church, and when she returned a few hours later she'd stopped talking."

"And how do you explain that?"

"Well, I examined her, unfortunately. She'd been torn to shreds."

"Raped?"

"In every way possible and imaginable. In my opinion, she'd run into some bad people during her night away. If she's not any better by tonight, I'll have her taken to Camporeale hospital."

"Did the signura tell you which church the girl had gone to?"

"The same one where they themselves go: San Cono."

Dr. Presti's stay in Palizzolo as substitute town doctor turned out not to be as long as Bellanca had expected.

In fact, it lasted only until eleven o'clock that morning, because at ten-thirty, the door of the holding cell opened and the captain said to the doctor:

"You're free to go. I've exonerated you of the charges. Have a good day."

He turned his back and went out. Bellanca was so surprised he didn't even say goodbye.

At more or less the same time of day, Lieutenant Villasevaglios went to don Anselmo Buttafava's house.

"It is my pleasure to inform you that Captain Montagnet has withdrawn the charges against you."

Having thought, upon seeing the lieutenant, that Villasevaglios had come to arrest him, don Anselmo very nearly fainted in relief.

At half past eleven, His Excellency Eustachio Benincasa, prefect of Camporeale, rang Mayor Calandro on the telephone. The mayor was so excited he immediately gushed with gratitude.

"Thank you so much, Your Excellency, for having so quickly intervened to rel—"

"Would you let me speak first, for the love of God?"

"My apologies, Your Excellency."

"I wanted to tell you that I just now received a petition signed by a hundred or so citizens of Palizzolo, demanding the release of Dr. Buzzanca . . . "

"Bellanca, Your Excellency."

"Yes, right, Bellanca. I'm telling you so that you can communicate to the signatories that my reply is to be patient for a few more days. Captain Montagnet is acting in a perfectly lawful manner to restore order in Palizzolo. And you, as mayor, must cooperate with him unconditionally. Have I made myself clear?"

"Perfectly clear, Your Excellency."

"What did you want to tell me?"

"Nothing, Your Excellency."

So it wasn't the prefect who'd ordered Montagnet to step back. And the captain was not the type of man to change his mind about any action of his own. Then the mayor remembered that Commendatore Padalino had said he would talk with the Honorable Barrafranca. It was possible Barrafranca had intervened immediately. The captain's surprise move made the mayor feel uneasy. He went out of his office, telling the usher he'd be right back. On mornings when the weather was good, the commendatore liked to sit out on the balcony of his home and watch the people passing by.

And there he was, in fact. Calandro called up to him from the street.

"Commendatore, have you heard the news?" he asked.

"That they let Bellanca out of jail? Yes."

"I want to thank the Honorable Barrafranca for—"

"But, Mr. Mayor, I wasn't able to talk to Ciccino."

Then why had Montagnet decided to release Dr. Bellanca?

'Ngilino the overseer pulled up at the Buttafava house just before midday. From the mule he unloaded rounds of *tuma*, *primosale*, and ricotta cheese, fruit, vegetables, pork sausages, a just-slaughtered suckling lamb, and four rabbits, and brought them into the larder. Then he went upstairs to don Anselmo's office.

"I beg your pardon for the other day, sir. But I'd just found out about Totina and felt like I was going crazy . . . "

"Why didn't you say anything to me at the time?"

"I was too ashamed. My wife told me you slapped Totina around a little. You were right."

"She's like a daughter to me."

"I know, don Anselmo."

"And you know what made me lose my head, 'Ngilì? She wouldn't give me a straight answer! She just pulled my leg and said it was the Holy Spirit that got her pregnant!"

"But, sir, with all due respect, you're wrong. She wasn't trying to pull your leg. She really believes it."

"Believes what?"

"That it was the Holy Spirit. She really means it."

"Has lost her mind?"

"No, sir, she's a normal girl. She just says it was the Holy Spirit."

"But what do you think? Have you any idea who it could have been?"

"None whatsoever. My wife's got no idea either. You see, Catarina never lets Totina out of her sight. We're scared, with all these criminals roaming round the countryside . . . . Totina's a beautiful girl and somebody might try and take advantage of her."

"So we're supposed to believe it was the Holy Spirit?"

'Ngilino shrugged.

"And what about when Catarina and Totina come into town for Mass on Sundays?" don Anselmo continued.

"Nah, she keeps 'er eye on 'er even worse than at San Giusippuzzo. Totina and Catarina get there early in the morning, say their confessions, and then take communion. Round four in the afternoon, they head back home to San Giusippuzzo."

"Wait a second," said don Anselmo. "And what do they do between the end of the Mass and four o'clock?"

"They go an' eat at my sister-in-law Clarizza's house. She's Catarina's big sister."

"And does this sister-in-law have any sons?"

"Yessir, she's got two. But they're in America."

"And how old is her husband?"

"'E's eighty. Turiddru was twenty years older than Clarizza when they got married."

There seemed to be no answer. Could it really have been the Holy Spirit?

At that moment the voice of the town crier rose up from the street.

"Citizens of Palizzolo!" he shouted in Italian, for anyone who might understand. "The state of martial law has ended! The curfew and prohibition of public assembly have also been lifted!"

This was immediately followed by the Sicilian translation:

"*Cumpaisani palizzoloti!* No more martial law! You can stay out all night if you like and get together with as many people as you want!"

*

At four o'clock that afternoon Casimiro the manservant intercepted the mayor as he was coming out of his home on his way to City Hall.

"Don Liborio asked if you could drop in at the club for a minute."

As soon as Mayor Calandro entered the salon, everyone present started clapping.

"Long live our mayor!" cried don Stapino Vassallo.

Almost all the members were there, even Dr. Bellanca, who hardly ever went to the club. Only Baron Lo Mascolo and Marquis Cammarata were missing.

"Are we all present?" President Spartà asked the secretary.

"All present except for the sick."

"Casimiro!" don Liborio called.

The waiter came in with four bottles of champagne fresh out of the icehouse. A small table had already been set in one corner of the great room and was covered with glasses. The bottles were uncorked and the glasses filled.

"Gentlemen, please serve yourselves," said don Liborio Spartà. "But first I should like to propose a toast of thanks to Mayor Calandro and all those who supported our initiative to free Dr. Bellanca. The pressure the mayor and all of us put on the prefect has achieved the desired result. To your health, Dr. Bellanca!"

They all drank. The mayor didn't feel like telling the truth, which was that the prefect had nothing whatsoever to do with the matter.

"Another round?" don Serafino Labianca asked.

"Of course!" said don Liborio. "Whom would you like to toast?"

"I propose a toast to the unfaithful wife of Captain Montagnet!"

Everyone laughed. At a certain point don Anselmo approached Dr. Bellanca, put an arm around his shoulders, and pulled him a short distance away from the others.

"There's something I wanted to ask you."

"Go right ahead."

Before speaking, don Anselmo pulled him even farther aside. He didn't want anyone to hear him.

"Can an eighty-year-old man get a girl pregnant?"

"Apparently there have been some such cases. But it's extremely rare. Why do you ask?"

"Because my overseer's daughter, Totina—"

"I know the whole story, don Anselmo. Her mother brought her to me for an examination."

"The only male that Totina could have had any contact with was Zia Clarizza's husband, but he's eighty years old."

"You're referring to Turiddru Cannizzaro?"

"Precisely."

"But do you know Cannizzaro?"

"No, sir."

"Cannizzaro is a patient of mine. He suffers from catarrh, but is otherwise a strong, healthy man."

"So in fact you're saying it *could* have been him!"

"Not on your life, don Anselmo! I didn't say that!"

"You just don't want to compromise yourself," don Anselmo said in disappointment.

And, sidling up to the lawyer Sciortino, he took him by the arm and pulled him aside.

"I would like you to draft a statement of denunciation for me, which I'll drop by later to sign."

"I'm at your service, don Anselmo. Whom do you want to denounce?"

"Captain Montagnet, for abuse of power."

"You can't do that, don Anselmo. It's true that the prefect has proved us right, but that would be pissing outside the pot!"

"Well, maybe you happen to piss outside the pot, seeing that your hands shake! And if your hands shake that bad, we can only imagine your cock!"

Sciortino decided it was best to turn his back and walk away. It was not a day for squabbling.

Signura Albasia Chiarapane arrived in Palizzolo from Salsetto. A woman of fifty, five-foot-eleven, and blonde, she had a baritone voice, was authoritarian and brusque in manner, and looked a little like an ostrich. Even Teresi felt a tad intimidated by her. She didn't even embrace her son and didn't bother to ask what had happened to him. Instead, she went immediately on the attack:

"What is this? All these days without any news from you? Is that any way to treat your mother?"

"Mamà . . . "

"You're just like your father! Both of with your heads in the clouds, and I always have to take care of everything!"

"Mamà . . . "

"What did you do to your lips?"

"Mamà . . . "

"I bet you didn't even go to the Cammaratas'!"

"Mamà . . . "

"The man you sent to Salsetto told me you had a bout of the flu. Well, it looks to me like you're all better. Now get dressed and let's go!"

"Mamà . . . "

"Signora, your son has suffered a concussion, lost three teeth, broken three ribs, and I don't know how many—"

"Didn't I just say he always has his head in the clouds? You went and got run over by a carriage!"

Luigino, her son, became disheartened, closing his eyes and lying down in bed. Teresi grabbed the enraged ostrich by the arm and dragged her into his study.

"And who are you, may I ask?" asked Signura Albasia.

"I'm Matteo Teresi, I'm a lawyer, and it was I who, together with my nephew Stefano, found your son on the street. He'd been savagely beaten, left for dead, put in a large sack, and dropped by the side of the road like an animal."

The lawyer made a point of telling her exactly what had happened, without diluting a thing. He wanted to make her as incensed as possible.

"And did Luigino recognize the assailant?"

"The assailants, Signora. There were two of them: a mafioso, and the Marquis Cammarata."

"I don't think this is any time for jokes! Shame on you! Marquis Cammarata is a gentleman who would never hurt a fly!"

"Just ask your son, Signora."

"But why would he do anything like that?"

"Because he's convinced Luigino got his eldest daughter, Paolina, pregnant, and that—"

The signora jumped out of her chair, dashed straight for the staircase, went upstairs, entered her son's room, and dealt him a hard slap in the mouth.

Blood immediately started flowing from the reopened wounds.

But the lad's mother didn't even notice.

"You disgusting cad! Taking advantage of my cousin's innocent daughter!"

"Grab her," Teresi said to his nephew.

And together they seized her and dragged her downstairs again to the study.

Teresi locked the door and put the key in his pocket.

"Now try to calm down, Signora. Your son spent the whole night in a state of delirium. I wrote down what he was saying. And you must know that people speak the truth when they're delirious."

He handed her a sheet of paper.

"Would you please read this?" he said.

*

Also at four o'clock that afternoon, Dr. Palumbo, seeing that Rosalia Pampina still wouldn't make up her mind to drink so much as a drop of water and insisted on remaining silent with her eyes popping out of her head, loaded her into the carriage with the help of the notary's wife and a maid, and took her to the hospital in Camporeale. There a doctor examined her and then said to his colleague from Palizzolo:

"I'm going to have to report this."

"So go ahead and report it," said Palumbo.

Half an hour later, the report, which described severe, repeated acts of sexual violence and sodomy inflicted by unknown parties upon the person of young Rosalia Pampina, residing in Palizzolo at the home of Domenico Giallonardo, notary, was brought to the attention of one Lieutenant Di Lullo, commanding officer of the Carabinieri station in Camporeale. The lieutenant then duly passed it on, according to protocol, to Captain Montagnet.

When the report arrived on the captain's desk, he was not surprised. He already knew Rosalia Pampina's story, having been told it by Lieutenant Villasevaglios, who had obtained the names of the three women raped by Salamone the brigand before letting them go free.

For the sake of investigative thoroughness, the captain dropped in at the Giallonardo home. The notary was out, but his wife, Signura Romilda, told him everything he wanted to know.

"But who could it have been?" Signura Romilda asked when she had finished. "She didn't tell us anything when she got back here. And it could only have happened during the night she spent out."

"Right," said the captain, refraining from telling her about the brigand.

He thanked her and left. But if Rosalia was speaking before she went to church, why did she stop when she got back from church? Of course it was possible that the trauma from the violence she'd suffered had a delayed onset. Or else, since she was a churchgoing girl, maybe when she went to confess, the priest hadn't wanted to grant her absolution? And if so, why deny her that?

The girl had not consented to the act—on the contrary, according to Villasevaglios, she had taken the whole thing much harder than the other two girls, and it had required a lot of effort to reassure her.

Captain Montagnet decided to go and speak directly with the priest of San Cono.

The first thing Patre Filiberto Cusa said was that all he could tell him about Rosalia Pampina was that she was a serious girl with a healthy fear of God who went to confession and took Communion every week.

"And did she confess the evening she came here?"

"That was her reason for coming."

"And did she tell you about the rape?"

"I can't answer you, as I'm sure you're well aware."

"One last question, Reverend. Did you grant her absolution?"

"You're very clever, Captain. If I answered your question, I would be implicitly admitting that Rosalia had confessed to something so dire as to jeopardize her chance of absolution. But I want to tell you something that might be of help to you. For us, no sin is committed if a person is forced to sin through violent coercion. I hope I'm being clear."

"Perfectly clear."

Therefore, Rosalia had been granted absolution. So then why had she fallen into despair? He had an idea.

"One more question, Father. How long was she here in church, do you remember?"

"I would say not more than twenty minutes."

There was something that didn't add up. Signura Giallonardo had told him that Rosalia returned home two hours after she'd gone out. Granting that she'd spent half an hour in church, where had she spent the other hour and a half? And, more importantly, with whom?

*

When the captain returned to the station, the carabiniere on duty told him there was a couple, a man and a woman, waiting to see him. He'd shown them into the captain's office. As Montagnet entered, the two stood up.

"Good afternoon. My name is Matteo Teresi, and I'm a lawyer here in town," said the man.

"And I am Signora Albasia Chiarapane."

"Pleased to meet you."

Sitting down he realized that he'd left the hospital doctor's report on his desk. He grabbed it and put it in a drawer, not knowing, however, that Teresi had had all the time in the world to commit it to memory.

"What can I do for you?"

The lawyer and the lady exchanged a glance of consultation. She went first.

"The lawyer and I are here to report the attempted murder of my son, Luigi."

"Did this happen here?"

"Yes."

"Is it an accusation against an unknown party?"

Now it was Teresi's turn to speak.

"No. We are accusing Marquis Filadelfo Cammarata and a noted local mafia chief known in town as *'u zù* Carmineddru, but whose surname is unknown to us."

"I know his surname," said the captain. "His name is Carmine Pregadio. And where is her son at present?"

"At my house," replied Teresi. "We picked him up off the street. They'd put him inside a sack, apparently thinking he was dead."

"I would like to hear his testimony first. Can he come here?"

"Doctor Palumbo, who has been attending to him, has forbidden him to get out of bed. But if you'd like to come to my house—"

"Let's go," said the captain, getting up.

*

After more than an hour, Teresi came out with the captain

and accompanied him to Dr. Palumbo's office, as Montagnet wanted to hear his testimony. As they were walking in silence, Teresi came out with an expression intended to prick the captain's curiosity.

"How odd, though!"

"What's odd?" asked Montagnet.

"That Baron Lo Mascolo's daughter is also two months pregnant!"

But he didn't seem so interested.

"He came charging over to my house," Teresi continued, "accusing my nephew of having seduced his daughter."

"Did he threaten him?"

"He wanted to shoot him dead!" the lawyer said, laughing.

"Threatening with a firearm. Would you like to press charges?"

"No. He was finally convinced it wasn't my nephew. But don't you find it strange that two unmarried girls are both exactly two months pregnant?"

"As far as that goes, the number of pregnant women who don't want to reveal the name of the culprit—for lack of a better term—is four."

Teresi was stunned, stopping dead in his tracks in the middle of the square. He didn't know that Dr. Presti, after half an hour of interrogation by the captain, spiced with the threat of a ten-year prison sentence, had cracked and told him everything he'd been told by Dr. Bellanca.

"But . . . how did you find out . . . ?"

"We're carabinieri, aren't we?"

He'd just dropped the captain off at Dr. Palumbo's and was on his way home, where Luigino's mother was waiting for him, when he was stopped by don Anselmo Buttafava.

"I have a request, my good man."

"I'm at your service, don Anselmo."

"I need you to draft an accusation for me . . . "

"I'm sorry, don Anselmo, but isn't Sciortino your regular lawyer?"

"Yes, and in fact I approached him first, but he wouldn't hear of it."

"Whom are you accusing?"

"Captain Montagnet, for abuse of power."

"That's a rather groundless accusation."

"You think? So his charge against me had deep foundations?"

"Listen, could we talk about this tomorrow morning at nine? I'll come to you, if you prefer."

"All right, I'll be waiting. Can I ask you one more thing?"

"I'm in a bit of a rush, don Anselmo. Go ahead."

"In your opinion, can an eighty-year-old man get a young girl pregnant?"

The lawyer froze in his tracks for the second time in ten minutes.

"Why are you asking me that?"

"Because Totina, the daughter of my farm overseer, 'Ngilino, is two months pregnant and saying it was the Holy Spirit that did it. But I think it was an uncle of hers, except for the fact that he's eighty years old. He must have taken advantage of her when she came into town for Holy Mass."

The lawyer was barely even listening to him anymore. He was wondering whether Totina was already one of the four pregnant girls, or the fifth.

Chapter VIII
Attorney Teresi Starts Thinking About Things

Signura Albasia Chiarapane headed back to Salsetto as the sun was setting, but before leaving announced that she would be back the following afternoon. After eating what his daytime housekeeper had made, and serving some as well to Luigino, Teresi told his nephew not to go upstairs to chat with the lad, but to come into his study.

"I want to ask you something."

"Go ahead."

"It's about Antonietta Lo Mascolo."

"I've already told you what I know about her. But if you want to keep talking about her, I can do that too."

"Stefanù, I've been giving this whole affair a lot of thought. You have maintained, and continue to maintain, that Antonietta was in no way the kind of girl who would drop her knickers for somebody she'd just met the day before, correct?"

"Correct. But not even for somebody she met three years before, either."

"I would like to know what it is that makes you so sure."

"It's the way she acts, Zio. The way she talks. And she wasn't just making small talk. She was convinced in her heart of everything she did and said. One time we even talked about when she would get married. She had a very clear idea of the kind of man she would choose: he had to be serious, and honest. Just like her. She didn't care whether he was rich or not. Last year the baron told her that Baron Piscopo's son, Arrigo, had expressed interest. She replied that it was completely out of the question. She'd seen this Arrigo once, and that had been enough."

"So you would rule out some secret boyfriend?"

"Absolutely. And I can also tell you that even if she had one, she would never make love to him until after they got married. I would bet my life on it."

"So the baron's reasoning concerning you wasn't incorrect."

"What do you mean?"

"That is, being the only man his daughter frequented and in whom she confided . . . "

"Yes, in that sense, he was right. But I've never touched Antonietta."

"Well, somebody did. And how!"

"But, Zio, where did it happen? How did he manage to persuade her? How did he find the time to be with her?'"

"You told me Antionietta was all church and hearth and home, right?"

"Right."

"And what did Luigino say to us about Paolina? Didn't he describe her with the same words as you just now did with Antonietta? Don't the two girls seem like carbon copies?"

"They are like carbon copies."

"And now let me tell you the story of a third girl I learned about on my way home. Her name is Totina, and she's the daughter of don Anselmo Buttafava's overseer. Like the others, she's also two months pregnant, and says the father is the Holy Spirit."

"What are you saying?" Stefano said in dismay.

"What I'm saying is true."

"An overseer's daughter!"

"As you can see, cocks don't care about class. Now, back to Totina. When she and her mother come to town for Sunday mass, the mother never lets her out of her sight. The only time the girl is alone is when she goes to confession. So, another case of a girl who's all church and hearth and home."

"But that doesn't seem to be of any help to us."

"Oh, it's a help, Stefanù, it's a big help!"

"How?"

"Let's think it through. If we rule out the possibility that these girls screwed up at home, what's left?"

"Church."

"There you go!"

"But, Zio, what's going through your head? How would it be possible to do anything like that in church?"

"Well, technically, it *is* possible, as far as that goes. Have you ever been, for example, at midnight mass on the last day of the year? It's so crowded you couldn't fit a pin in there! And that was how my friend Gegè Pirrotta fucked his girlfriend the first time! Standing up, right there in church!"

"Zio, I think you're letting your imagination run away with you. Here we're talking about three women who—"

"Four."

"What do you mean, four?" Stefano asked in shock.

"There are four of them, all two months pregnant. Montagnet told me."

"And who's the fourth?"

"He didn't tell me her name."

"All right, but can you imagine four women, in four different churches but on the same occasion, letting someone lift their skirts without making a peep? Your friend's case was a little different, he and the girl were a couple. But I can assure you that Antonietta did not have a secret boyfriend. Nor did Paolina, I don't think."

"As far as you know."

"Of course, as far as I know!"

"What if it was just one man?"

"But, Zio! Are you trying to tell me there's some magic dick wandering from church to church?! Whether it was one man or four, the girls would have rebelled just the same!"

"Maybe they didn't open their mouths because they were ashamed of what was happening to them."

"Knowing Antonietta as well as I do, I think she would have started screaming so loud they would've heard her all the way to Palermo!"

"All right, let's make another hypothesis. I never go to church, and neither do you. However, the last time a procession went by, I saw that it wasn't just old and young women and old men behind San Cono, there were also middle-aged and young men. Some of them were wearing rosettes in their lapels."

"That's the symbol of the congregation of San Cono."

"And who are the ones with the cowls on Good Friday?"

"They're the congregation of the Passion."

"Do you see what I'm getting at? There isn't a single church that doesn't have its congregation. And they are composed of more or less young men who go to those churches. Who share the same devout sentiments as Antonietta, Paolina and Totina. Who share spiritual interests. Isn't it possible that one of the girls could have a secret lover among these men?"

"But I've already told you, Zio, that before she's married, Antonietta will never—"

"But how do you know they're not already married?" Teresi asked, wild-eyed.

"Married? Without anyone knowing?"

"What need is there to tell anyone? They could have got married in secret before God! In their minds and consciences they're married! And in that case Antonietta could very well make love with the man she considered her husband!"

"And where would they have consummated the marriage, in your opinion? On the main altar?"

Teresi didn't answer.

"I'm a little tired," said Stefano, getting up. "I'm gonna go talk to Luigino a little and then go to bed. Good night."

But Teresi did not have a good night. He spent three quarters of it in his study, racking his brains and taking notes.

*

The chief clerk at the registry office of Palizzolo, Cosimo Spartipane, opened the office at eight o'clock sharp, as he did every morning except weekends and holidays. He went in, doffed his hat, bent down to open the bottom drawer of his desk, where he kept his pen and ink pot, and when he stood back up, he found Captain Montagnet before him. He nearly had a heart attack. First, because, though he was a perfectly honest man, the mere sight of a carabiniere always scared him to death. And, second, because he hadn't heard him come in.

"Good morning," said the captain.

"Good morning. Do you need something?"

"Yes. Two family status certificates."

"For whom?"

"For Baron Alfonso Lo Mascolo and Marquis Filadelfo Cammarata."

"I'm not sure whether regulations allow—"

"As you may have gathered, I am not requesting them for my own personal pleasure. I need them for an investigation. And I don't think family status certificates are confidential. Therefore . . . Unless you intend to put up an obstruction, in which case—"

"When do you need them by?"

"Within the hour."

As soon as Montagnet left, Spartipane dashed into the office of the mayor, who had just arrived.

"The captain wants the family status certificates for Cammarata and Lo Mascolo!"

"Why?"

"How should I know?"

Want to bet that Montagnet was itching again to throw someone in jail? Perhaps it was best to alert both men, the marquis and the baron, of this new development. The mayor wrote two identical notes in which he changed only the name of the addressee, and sent them off with two municipal policemen in two open envelopes, so that the policemen could read them and tell everyone in town about the captain's latest move.

*

At nine o'clock that morning Teresi came knocking at don Anselmo's door and was immediately shown into his office.

"So, as I was saying yesterday evening, I would like to denounce Captain Montagnet for . . . " don Anselmo began, trailing off when he saw the lawyer raise his hand.

"I spent all light researching whether there were any legal precedents," said the lawyer.

This was a big fat lie, but Teresi had no reason for wanting to turn Montagnet against him. But neither did he want to displease don Anselmo.

"Why the hell should I care about precedents?"

"You may not care, but we lawyers do! And I have to tell you that I found no precedents for this kind of case."

"Oh, yeah? So if someone steals my shit, I can't do anything about it because nobody has stolen anyone's shit before?"

"Your comparison is not exactly apropos, don Anselmo. The fact is that the captain has been acting in accordance with the powers granted him by the state of emergency."

"And has the state of emergency been lifted?"

"It has."

"Then why doesn't this goddamn captain get the hell out of

our hair instead of going around and asking left and right for everybody's family status certificates?"

"Everybody who?"

"Everybody like Baron Lo Mascolo and Marquis Cammarata, for example."

"And when did he request them?"

"Somebody came and told me just a minute before you got here."

What could this mean? Teresi would give this some thought later.

"That's why, don Anselmo, I'm sorry I can't help you. But I do think I could be some use to you in Totina's case."

"Really?"

"Yes. I would need to talk to—"

"The girl isn't talking; all she says is that it was the Holy Spirit that did it."

"All I would need is five minutes with her mother."

Don Anselmo took his watch out of his pocket.

"Are you free at five o'clock this afternoon?"

"Yes."

"Then come back at five, and Catarina will be here."

The explanation for Montagnet's requesting the family status certificates came to Teresi as he was eating a morning cannolo at the Cafè Esperia. Dropping the cannolo halfway through, he dashed back home.

There he found Stefano and Luigino chatting and laughing.

"Stefanù, do you know exactly how old Antonietta is?"

"Seventeen years and seven months old."

"And how old is Paolina?" Teresi asked Luigino.

"Sixteen and a half. Why do you ask?"

"Because they're both minors, that's why!"

Then he got into his carriage and galloped off to Camporeale, where he had to argue a case in court.

*

And so he missed the greatest spectacle ever seen in Palizzolo.

At ten-thirty that morning, two carabinieri corporals and one marshal, led by Lieutenant Villasevaglios, who was looking even taller and thinner than usual—looking indeed like death itself on the march—left their compound and headed towards the center of town. Feeling curious, a few layabouts started following them. When the carabinieri reached the main square, the number of rubberneckers doubled. In short, by the time the carabinieri turned onto Via Cammarata, there were some fifty people behind them. Lieutenant Villasevaglios knocked on the great door. They went inside. The door closed. Taking advantage of the pause, a few people ran off in search of other townfolk.

Then, all at once, despite the fact that all the windows were closed, a terrible buzz of voices burst forth inside the palazzo, shouts, wails, cries that could be heard all the way down in the street.

Then the door opened, and out came, in the following order: Lieutenant Villasevaglios, the carabinieri marshal, the Marquis Filadelfo Cammarata in handcuffs, and, bringing up the rear, the two carabinieri corporals. The marquis's face was green and he was trembling like a leaf. But clearly it was not from fear or shame, but from rage. The instant he came out the door, all the windows on the front of the palazzo opened suddenly, and seven of the marquis's eight daughters appeared, shouting and cursing at the carabinieri.

At that exact moment the marquis leapt forward and in a flash sunk his teeth into the ear of the marshal in front of him, not letting go until the lieutenant, having unsheathed his sword, whacked him in the head with the side of it.

It was estimated that some two hundred people accompanied the carabinieri to the station.

Less than fifteen minutes later, the lawyer Sciortino arrived. He was greeted by Lieutenant Villasevaglios.

"Mind telling me what my client is charged with?"

"Attempted murder, in complicity with Signor Carmine Pregadio."

"Have you also arrested Pregadio?"

"He has fled and is at large."

"And whom did they try to kill?"

"A young man by the name of Luigi Chiarapane."

"And why?"

"I don't know the answer to that question."

*

At noon there was a special meeting at the castle of the Duke Ruggero d'Altomonte, attended by all the nobility of Palizzolo, namely: Marquis Spinotta, Baron Piscopo, Baron Roccamena, and Baron Lo Mascolo (who had gone out of his house for the first time since the start of the confusion, owing to the gravity of the situation). Unavoidably absent was the Marquis Cammarata.

The meeting was held in the duke's bedroom. The duke sat in an armchair with a heavy woolen blanket over his legs. At a hundred and two years of age, he was always cold. And continuously talking to himself.

"There is no more religion!"

"There is no more respect!"

"There is no more order!"

"There are no more manners!"

"What have we come to?"

"A marquis handcuffed like a common delinquent!"

"Held up to public ridicule!"

"To the mockery of the low-born rabble!"

When the duke had finished his rant, Marquis Spinotta said that they had to prevent the captain from doing any more harm.

"Can he do any more than he's done?" asked Baron Lo Mascolo.

"Absolutely!" replied Baron Piscopo. "And his next victim will be you!"

"Me?!"

"Yes, sir, you! Did you know that Montagnet has asked to see your family status certificate?"

"Yes, I know. But why did he do that?"

"How should I know? The fact remains that he requested the Cammarata certificate and then immediately arrested the marquis. Therefore . . . "

Baron Lo Mascolo turned pale.

"What sort of rapport do you have with your cousin, the duke of San Loreto?"

Duke Simone Loreto di San Loreto was the highest functionary of the court of His Majesty the King.

"I have an excellent rapport with him. Why do you ask?"

"Could you ring him in Rome and describe to him the situation that has developed here? If the duke could just say a few words to the General Commander of the Carabinieri . . . "

"I can try," said Marquis Spinotta.

At that moment Duke Ruggero d'Altomonte opened his mouth to speak.

"Friends . . . "

Since he spoke in only the faintest of voices, everyone drew near to listen.

"Would you like to know who's to blame for all this?"

Amidst the respectful silence of everyone present, the duke, after taking a short breath, pronounced his verdict:

"It's all the fault of the French Revolution!"

*

Teresi wasn't at the Camporeale courthouse more than half

an hour, because the hearing was postponed. The hospital was right next door to the courthouse.

Without thinking twice, he decided to go and inquire about the condition of the girl who had been raped, the one mentioned in the doctor's deposition he had read while waiting for Captain Montagnet. Her story was of interest to him as a journalist. He wanted to write an article about it. Luckily he remembered her name.

"My name is Stefano Torrisi," he said to the nun at the entrance desk. "I would like some news about a relative of mine."

"What is her name?"

"Rosalia Pampina."

Why did the nun seem a little awkward?

"I don't know whether . . . Well, please take a seat in the waiting room."

After a short wait, a doctor in a white coat came in.

"Signor Torrisi?"

There were three men in the room, and none of them moved.

"Is there a Signor Torrisi here?" the doctor asked again.

All at once Teresi remembered he'd given the receptionist that name.

"I'm sorry," he said, standing up. "My mind was elsewhere."

"Please follow me," said the doctor.

He led him into an office, sat him down, and closed the door.

"In what way were you related to Rosalia Pampina?"

Were related? Why didn't he say "*are* related"?

"I'm a second cousin. Why do you ask?"

"Because Rosalia Pampina committed suicide at dawn this morning, throwing herself out a fourth-floor window. My deepest condolences."

"But . . . wasn't anyone keeping an eye on her?"

"Why should we have been keeping an eye on her? Yesterday evening we had the impression her condition was starting to improve."

"In what sense?"

"She spoke. She made a perfectly comprehensible statement, even though the meaning was a little obscure."

"What did she say?" the lawyer asked, feeling, for reasons unknown, a lump in his throat. As if Rosalia really were a relation of his.

"She said: 'The penance is like the sin.' And she repeated it twice. Then fell back into her catatonic state. But there's a problem you could perhaps help us with."

"What is it?"

"We've been unable to inform her family because we have no address for them. Are you from Palizzolo?"

"Yes."

"All right, then, if you could inform Dr. Palumbo, I'm sure he could—"

"I'll do so at once."

*

The penance is like the sin. What could it mean? Why not discuss it with Montagnet? Two heads might stand a better chance of grasping the meaning.

He dropped in at the printworks where they published the newssheet he edited and wrote, which came out once a week.

"We're still missing the lead article," said the printer. "And if you don't send me something by tomorrow, or day after tomorrow at the latest, we'll have to come out late."

Teresi headed back to Palizzolo, but when he got there he found some fifty people still gathered outside the carabinieri station.

"What's going on?"

"The Marquis Cammarata's been arrested."

He turned around and went to inform Dr. Palumbo of the death of Rosalia Pampina.

CHAPTER IX
WHAT'S TWO PLUS TWO?

The investigating magistrate, Artidoro Tommasino, arrived in Palizzolo at the break of dawn and set up shop in a room at the carabinieri compound, along with the court clerk he'd brought with him.

First he sat and spoke face to face with the captain, and then he sent a carriage to fetch Luigino Chiarapane. He listened to the young man for an hour, then sent him home again.

After this, he sent for Dr. Palumbo and drew up a report of all the wounds the doctor had found on the lad's body.

And after this he had Stefano, Teresi's nephew, brought in and asked him to describe how they had happened to find Luigino inside a sack, and what they had done as soon as they realized the youth was still alive.

Then, to everyone's surprise, he sent for Teresi.

The moment he saw him enter the building, the lawyer Sciortino, who was standing outside the judge's room, went in together with Teresi.

"Which of you is Matteo Teresi?" asked the judge.

"I am," said Teresi.

"And who are you?"

"My name is Sciortino, and I'm also a lawyer and represent the Marquis Cammarata. I am here to file a formal protest."

"Why?"

"Because you are seeking the help of the accuser's lawyer, while the case is still in the investigative stages!"

"For your information, I am not seeking the help of anyone! And I refuse to consider your statement any further! I have not summoned Matteo Teresi here in his capacity as the accuser's lawyer, but as a witness. You can verify this later, when you read the minutes of our meeting. Now leave this room at once!"

Upon hearing the news of the marquis's arrest, Teresi had congratulated the captain in his mind for having had the courage to do such a thing; he was thus now further delighted to learn that Judge Tommasino wasn't afraid of anyone.

As soon as Sciortino left, the judge began speaking.

"Let me start by saying, as I have just said, that you are here solely as a witness. Your nephew, Stefano, told me how you managed to find young Chiarapane on the street. He said he'd wanted to take him to the nearest house, which was Palazzo Cammarata, and that you were against this and brought him instead to your house. Is this correct?"

"Yes, that's correct."

"Then my question is: Why?"

Teresi hadn't been expecting this dangerous question, and had a moment of hesitation.

"I don't quite understand," he said to buy time.

"Your nephew was very clear on the matter. He told us that when he'd suggested taking the injured young man to Palazzo Cammarata, you replied, saying, in so many words, that you didn't want to give the marquis the chance to finish the job. So my question is quite simple: Since you had never seen that young man before and therefore knew nothing about him, what made you think at once that he would be risking his life by returning to the Cammarata home?"

The question was truly dangerous. If Teresi said he knew that the marquis was not to be trusted and had voted against his entry into the club, the judge might get the wrong idea. In the meantime, however, Teresi remembered what he'd been thinking when he found the young man in a sack on the street.

"Your honor, it was intuition, pure and simple, but still based on certain known patterns of behavior. You see, Stefano told me he thought the lad was a nephew of the marquis and often went to Palazzo Cammarata. Bear in mind that whoever beat the young man up believed him already dead. They then wrapped the body up in the sack and tossed it out just a few hundred yards away from Palazzo Cammarata. It was a precise message. A Mafia message. A corpse dumped far enough away from Palazzo Cammarata to rule out any suspicion that the Cammaratas were in any way involved. And I also remembered that the marquis had often been quick to solicit the services of the local Mafia chieftain, Carmine Pregadio, known as *'u zù* Carmineddru. That's all."

After dismissing Teresi, the judge summoned Marquis Cammarata. Since the marquis was still under arrest, he was flanked by a marshal and an unranked carabiniere, who stood on either side of his chair.

The marshal's ear was wrapped in a bandage.

"Did you injure yourself?" the judge asked.

"No, this man here bit me."

"So we must add the charge of resisting arrest and assaulting an officer of the law."

"I don't give a flying fuck," said the marquis, whose face was now sea-green.

"Listen, my lord marquis, you've been accused of attempted murder. What have you got to say for yourself?"

"That I did it, and you should stop busting my balls."

"Please have the accused's attorney come in," the judge said to the two guards.

The lawyer entered.

"Marquis, would you kindly repeat what you just said to me?"

"I said it was I who tried to kill that little son of a bitch."

Attorney Sciortino's heart sank into his shoes.

An hour later, Marquis Filadelfo Cammarata, now in chains "due to the dangerousness of the detainee," was taken to the prison of Camporeale.

*

At three o'clock that afternoon, with the authorization granted him by Judge Tommasino in hand, Captain Montagnet knocked on the great door of Palazzo Lo Mascolo.

"There's a carabinieri captain here wants to talk to you," Filippa the housekeeper said to the baron.

Don Fofò got worried. Not only did he not want to see so much as the shadow of Captain Montagnet, he also hadn't forgotten the words of Marquis Spinotta: "His next victim will be you!" And this time the could not escape out the back window, as he'd done at Teresi's house. There was nothing to be done.

Calati junco ca passa la china,[2] he reminded himself. Then he said to Filippa:

"Show him into the office—actually, no. Show him into the salon."

In the salon hung the painted portraits of some twenty ancestors; they would let the captain know who he was dealing with. Don Fofò took off his dressing gown, and as he was getting dressed his wife, the Baroness Marianna, arrived in a flurry.

Already when they got married the baroness wasn't exactly a raving beauty. But now, between the aging process and her anguish over their daughter Antonietta, she'd become frighteningly ugly. She took one look at Fofò and started crying.

[2] A Sicilian saying, the literal translation of which is: "Bend, reed, until the spate passes." It means, basically, "give in to adverse cirumstances while awaiting better times."

"They're going to take you to jail! I just know it! This time you're going to end up in jail!"

The baron pushed her aside with one hand, and with the other he grabbed his cojones firmly, to ward off back luck, then left the room, descended the stairs, and went into the salon.

The captain, who was standing and looking at the family portraits, gave the military salute and handed him a document. Don Fofò felt his heart sink. It was surely an arrest warrant. He started sweating as the room began to spin around him.

"I haven't got my glasses," he said, worried that his voice was trembling.

"Shall I read it for you?"

"Yes."

The captain read it.

When he'd finished, the baron very nearly embraced him. He was not going to jail after all, at least not this time. And he was especially glad not to be going to jail because of his slut of a daughter, whom he alternately considered dead and then alive but a slut. He decided to put up a little resistance, for form's sake, only to give in at once.

"If I've understood correctly, you are authorized to question my daughter, Antonietta, in the presence of her mother."

"That's correct."

"May I ask why you wish to speak with my daughter? And why in the presence of her mother? Because, on top of everything else, my daughter is sick in bed."

"My good baron, I could have sent two carabinieri here to bring your daughter in for questioning. Out of respect for your feelings as her father, I didn't do that."

So the captain knew that Antonietta was pregnant! His "feelings as her father" couldn't mean anything else. Therefore there was no need to playact any longer with him.

"I appreciate your courtesy, but you haven't answered my question."

"I shall do so at once. Your daughter is a minor, Baron. And I need to know whether she was the victim of a rape or a consenting partner. And I must proceed in the presence of her mother precisely because she is a minor."

Courteous but firm. On top of everything else, if the captain succeeded in making Antonietta talk, the whole thing could prove useful. The baron would find out the lover's name.

"All right," he said, leaving the room.

*

One hour later, the captain was knocking on the great door of Palazzo Cammarata.

"Bastard! Son of a bitch! Bugger!" the marquise started shouting as soon as she saw him.

And the seven daughters, including a tiny little girl who to the naked eye looked to be barely five years old, repeated in chorus:

"Bastard! Son of a bitch! Bugger!"

While the maids, from the kitchen, echoed:

" . . . ugger!"

Luckily Sciortino the lawyer was there in the house and was able to bring the situation under control and calm the marquise down. And so the captain was able to speak with the underage pregnant girl.

*

At five o'clock sharp, Teresi showed up at don Anselmo's house.

"Catarina is here."

"Don Anselmo, I'd like to ask a favor of you."

"Go ahead."

"I would like to speak with Catarina alone."

"Why can't I be present too?" asked don Anselmo, feeling offended.

"Because there may be some things she won't want to say to me with her boss present. Please do me this favor. It's in your own interest."

"All right, as you wish. Please go into my office, and I'll send her straightaway."

"I din't do nothin'," said Catarina as soon as she came in.

She was scared to death. Her hands were trembling.

"Nobody's saying you did anything."

"Are you a lawyer?"

"Yes."

Catarina started crying and shouting:

"Oh my God, my God, I'm done for! Oh the pain and trouble! Jesus, Mary and Joseph, take pity on my unhappy soul!"

"Why are you acting this way?"

"'Cause don Anselmo wants to take me to court!"

"What on earth is going through your head? Why would he want to take you to court!"

"'Cause I din't watch over my daughter and now she went and got pregnant!"

"Listen, Catarina. Don Anselmo can't do anything to you, believe me. Anyway, I'm not here as a lawyer, but as don Anselmo's friend."

"Really?"

"Really."

"No papers wit' writing on them?"

"No papers."

The woman calmed down a little.

"What do you want to know?"

"I'd like to try to find out who got your daughter pregnant."

"She says it was the Holy Spirit."

"Listen, the Holy Spirit is a spirit. Which means he doesn't have a body, do you understand? I want you to tell me what the two of you do on Sundays, after you go to Mass."

"We go an' eat at my sister's place."

"And do you stay at your sister's until four o'clock?"

"Sometimes . . . sometimes . . . "

Teresi felt a kind of tingling along his spine. He pretended not to be too interested, lighting a cigar and taking a few puffs.

"So, you were saying that sometimes . . . "

"Sometimes, right after we eat, she goes back to the church. But I take her there."

"And do you stay and wait for her?"

"No sir. She says: 'Mamà, come back an' get me in about a hour or hour an' a half.' An' so that's what I do."

Teresi, choking on his cigar smoke, started coughing.

"Now listen. When you go back to get her, are there sometimes other people with her?"

"Bah . . . sometimes there's another girl."

"How about boys?"

"Boys? Never!"

"And has Totina sometimes stayed at the church for more than an hour or hour and a half?"

"No, not at the church. But there was that time when they went on a retreat for a half a day."

*

On his way to the carabinieri station to talk to the captain, Teresi couldn't get the words Rosalia had said to the hospital doctor out of his head. *The penance is like the sin.*

And all at once the meaning of those words flashed before him, blinding and paralyzing him to the point that he almost got run over by a carriage. He recovered only because he'd managed for a moment to obliterate that meaning from his mind. He didn't want to believe it.

*

"If you've come here to talk to me about Marquis Cammarata, you know as well as I, Signor Teresi, that the matter is no longer in my hands," the captain said, to stay on the safe side.

"That's not why I came. And I thank you for agreeing to see me."

"What can I do for you?"

"Have you been informed that Rosalia Pampina committed suicide this morning at dawn?"

"Oh my God, no," said Montagnet. "The poor girl!"

He looked intently at Teresi.

"But how did you find out about this unlucky young woman?"

"I committed an indiscretion."

"Did you read the report I'd left on my desk?"

"Yes. I'm also a journalist, you know."

"I know. I read your articles, to keep myself informed. It's part of my job."

"Just to keep yourself informed?"

The captain pretended not to have heard, and kept on talking.

"That girl . . . Rosalia . . . was kidnapped and repeatedly raped by the brigand Salamone. She was freed by Lieutenant Villasevaglios, but apparently she never—"

"First," said Teresi.

"I'm sorry, I don't understand."

"First she was raped by the brigand Salamone, and then, when she felt guilty about it, she requested permission to confess her sins to a priest."

"I know. I spoke to her parish priest."

"And what did he tell you?"

"He said she arrived just as he was closing the church, insisted that she make a confession, and then left after she'd done this. But according to my research, she did not go straight back home, but returned about an hour and a half later. Since the woman she works for told me that as of that moment she no longer said a word and didn't want to eat or drink anything, there are two possibilities: either she didn't really start feeling the effects of the outrage done to her until after the confession, or, on her way home, had another unpleasant encounter that proved fatal to her."

"*Tertium non datur*?"[3] asked the lawyer.

"I don't see how . . . "

"Captain, the hospital doctor told me that just the night before, Rosalia had seemed to be improving, to the point that she began to speak again. She repeated twice, in dialect, a statement that I'll translate for you: 'the penance is like the sin.'"

Montagnet looked at him, not knowing what to say.

"The penance is like the sin," he repeated softly.

Then he understood.

He bolted upright and suddenly lost all his Piedmontese military aplomb.

"Oh, shit!" he said.

Then he sat back down and ran his hand over his brow.

"You must excuse me," he said, slightly embarrassed at having uttered an obscenity. "If you don't mind . . . " he said, undoing his tie and unfastening the top button of his shirt.

"Actually, that's not all I have to tell you," Teresi resumed. "A short while ago I spoke to the mother of one of the mysteriously pregnant girls."

"Who?"

[3] Is there no third possibility? (Lat. loc.)

"Her name is Totina; she's the daughter of don Anselmo Buttafava's overseer."

"Ah, yes, I know."

"Every Sunday Totina comes into town to attend Mass and then, afterwards, she sometimes goes back to the church and spends some time alone with the priest. She says her baby was conceived by the intercession of the Holy Spirit."

"More or less the same thing the other two girls I questioned today said," the captain observed. "One of them told me it was the will of God, and the other said that the fruit of her womb was willed by the Lord."

"So, then, Captain, shall we add things up? All of these pregnant girls assiduously frequented their respective churches. The only men they ever met with face to face were their priests. So, what's in the *cavagna*?"

"What is a *cavagna*?"

"It's a small wicker basket shaped like a cannolo but closed at one end, whose only purpose is to contain a small amout of ricotta cheese. So let's try again, Captain. What's in the *cavagna*?"

"Ricotta," Montagnet replied through clenched teeth.

"So we agree," said Teresi. "But we have no proof."

"But there *is* something we could do, just to get started," said the captain. "The overseer's daughter is also two months pregnant, isn't she?"

"Yes."

"Like the other three."

"Have you questioned the fourth girl as well?"

"No. She's a legal adult. The matter is out of my hands. And I can't tell you her name. But there is a very specific question we must ask: What happened in the churches of Palizzolo two months ago?"

"If we could only find out . . . "

Montagnet had an idea. He got up, opened the door, and went out. He returned five minutes later.

"I've just spoken with Marshal Sciabbarrà."

"Is he going to conduct an investigation?"

"Unofficially. A sort of home-cooked investigation. His wife is very devout and goes to church every day."

"I'm sorry, Captain, but if his wife is so devout, maybe she's not the right person for the task."

"No, I think she's fine. She's fifty years old and she's . . . not very attractive."

"Let's assume the woman tells us what happened. Surely she will not have been present when it happened. So we will have an additional element, but still no concrete proof."

"That's true. But I don't think it's going to be so easy to find any concrete proof."

"So we'll have nothing to show for our efforts."

"Perhaps we should do something to alarm the culprits and then await their next move. Know what I mean?"

"Perfectly. But what can we do to alarm them?"

Montagnet gave a sly smile.

"You're a journalist, aren't you?"

"Wait a second. If I write what's really been happening I'll be hit with at least eight or nine lawsuits for libel."

"But who ever said you should write what's really been happening? It's up to you and your skill to hint, make allusions, let it be surmised that . . . You journalists are masters at that sort of thing. The point is to set the alarm bells ringing, that's all."

This was also true. There was a knock at the door, and Marshal Sciabbarrà came in and gave a military salute. Only the captain asked questions.

"Did you speak with your wife?"

"Yes, sir."

"What did she tell you?"

"She said she'd heard mention, but she couldn't remember by whom, that there'd been a select gathering at the Benedictine convent, which has been empty for the past year."

"Did this event take place two months ago?"

"More or less."

"What was its purpose?"

"It was a kind of award given to the most devout women of the parish."

"What did it involve?"

"A half day of spiritual exercises conducted by the priests from the parishes in town."

"And did the priests have the convent reopened for the specific purpose of this gathering?"

"Yes, sir."

"Can you tell me anything else?"

"No, sir."

"Forgive me, but I must ask you a personal question, Marshal."

"Yes, sir."

"How is it that your wife, who seems to me an extremely devout woman, wasn't invited to this gathering?"

"The gathering was limited to young women only, married and unmarried, between the ages of sixteen and twenty-five."

Chapter X
The Lawyer Lays a Trap

Teresi left the station well after Vespers had rung, and headed for Piazza Garibaldi, where the church of San Cono stood. When he got there the church door was already locked. He looked at his watch: almost seven o'clock. It was just then starting to get dark. The parish priest, Don Filiberto Cusa, had told the captain that Rosalia arrived just as he was closing up, and that she'd left just after confessing herself. Calculating that she'd taken half an hour to tell the priest what Salamone the brigand had done to her, it must still have been light outside when she came out. This made it unlikely she'd run into any troublemakers, as the captain had conjectured. That wasn't yet the hour for troublemakers to come out on the street. There were still too many people about at that time of day; all those who had fled because of the cholera scare were returning. The house of Giallonardo the notary was barely fifty yards away.

The grocery shop directly opposite the church was still open, and a man, perhaps the owner, was sitting on a wicker chair right beside the entrance . . .

Perhaps he was also there the same accursed evening Rosalia went into the church? There was no harm in asking. He had nothing to lose. The sign over the shop entrance said: GERARDO PACE GROCER.

"Good evening, Signor Pace."

"Good evening," the man replied, looking confused.

There was nobody inside the store. On the counter Teresi

saw three or four rounds of tumazzo and other cheeses, including a caciocavallo. It must have been a house specialty.

"I'm looking for some caciocavallo di Ragusa. My good friend Giallonardo, the notary, just told me you might have some."

The man stood up. He was fat and sweaty.

"Of course I've got some. I'm the only person in town who's got it."

He went into the store, with Teresi following behind.

"How much would you like?"

It was best to get on his good side.

"A whole round, if that's all right."

Gerardo Pace's eyes glistened. He probably didn't do a great deal of business. Clearly this lone sale would make up for the whole day.

As the grocer was weighing the cheese, Teresi was racking his brains trying to figure out a way to broach the subject. But then Gerardo Pace asked him a question that took him by surprise.

"Do you know if there's any news about Rosalia?"

Since Teresi had said he was a close friend of the notary, it only stood to reason that . . .

"I'm very fond of that girl," the shopowner continued. "She does all her food shopping here. What do they say at the hospital?"

"They're not saying anything yet."

"I knew it was probably something serious! I walked her back to the notary's house after I saw her come out of the church."

"You saw her come out of the church in front?"

"She didn't really come out of the front door, but out the little door to the side, the one that leads to the sacristy. And, believe me, the girl couldn't stand up! And she wouldn't talk. I asked her over and over: 'What's wrong, Rosalì?' And she'd say nothing! Poor kid, I felt so bad for her!"

"Do you remember what time it was?"

"It was probably round eight-twenty, something like that, 'cause I always close at eight-thirty, and I remember that after I walked her home, I came back here and closed up. Will you be needing anything else?"

"Yes," Teresi said on impulse. "Another whole round, this time of sweet provolone. And give me that leg of prosciutto as well."

"But how are you going to carry all this stuff? Want me to help you carry it home?"

Signor Pace would have attracted more attention than a brass band, walking him home with so much food.

"Tell you what. Please wrap it all up for me, I'll pay for it, and tomorrow morning my nephew will drop by and pick it all up. But tell me something. Where does Don Filiberto Cusa live?"

"He's got three rooms above the sacristy. There's a wooden staircase leading straight up there from the sacristy."

*

"Do you know Don Filiberto Cusa?" Teresi asked Stefano as they were eating with Luigino, who by now was getting up out of bed whenever he felt like it. Dr. Palumbo had said that he could go home to Salsetto in two days' time.

"No. He doesn't know me and I don't know him. Who is he?"

"The priest of San Cono parish. Do you know at least where the church is?"

"Yes, that I know."

"Good. Do you have a piece of black cloth?"

"I think so."

"Good. Cut a strip of it and sew it onto the left sleeve of your jacket."

"Mourning?"

"Yes indeed. And if you have a black tie, put that on, too."

"So I'm in mourning."

"Yes, you are."

"So who died?"

"Your cousin, Rosalia Pampina, the daughter of your mother's sister. She killed herself while she was staying at the hospital."

"Why'd the poor thing kill herself?"

Teresi told him everything about the girl, and even told him about the talk he'd had with the grocer.

"What Pace told me confirms the captain's and my suspicions. Rosalia suffered two sexual aggressions: first at the hands of the brigand Salamone, and second, at the hands of Patre Filiberto Cusa."

"Inside the church?" asked Stefano, who couldn't bring himself to believe it.

"I found out that you can go upstairs to the priest's apartment directly from the sacristy. He must have taken her home."

"And what do you want me to say to the priest, all dressed up in mourning?"

"I want you to wait for him to finish saying the Mass, then go into the sacristy and, observing him very carefully, tell him that Rosalia killed herself. Once he's swallowed this news, you must tell him you want to talk to him in private, in a safe place, because you have something important to tell him. Try to get him to take you upstairs to his apartment. Then, when you're alone, you'll reveal to him that the night before she threw herself out the window, Rosalia talked to you and told you everything. And say there was also a nurse present."

"Then what?"

"Then you'll blackmail him. You'll say that, for starters, he must give you two thousand lire."

"And what if the guy's innocent and calls the carabinieri?"

"He won't, rest assured. If, at any rate, that were to happen, I'll explain the whole thing to Captain Montagnet."

At this point Luigino, who hadn't uttered a word throughout, said:

"I want to go with Stefano."

"And who will you be?"

"I'll be the nurse who heard what Rosalia said to her cousin. I'll be Stefano's accomplice. That way it'll all be more believable, I'm sure of it."

"All right," Teresi consented.

"And at what time should we go to the church?"

"At six in the morning, for the first Mass."

"Shit, why so early?"

"Because it's dangerous, Stefano. If, for example, Signora Giallonardo in the meantime goes and tells the priest that Rosalia is dead, we're screwed. Ah, and since there'll be two of you, there's a grocery shop right in front of the church, and I want you go there to pick up a round of caciocavallo and another of provolone, and a leg of prosciutto."

*

At a quarter to six the following morning, the two young men left the house to go to church. Teresi accompanied them to an appointed intersection. He was too nervous to sit tight at home waiting for them; it would have driven him crazy.

He went to the Burruano pastry shop and scarfed down three ricotta cannoli fresh out of the oven. In fact he'd wanted to eat only one, but the aroma was so heavenly he couldn't resist. When he came back out he had the feeling that if someone stuck a finger down his throat, they would touch the creamy ricotta with which he'd filled his stomach.

If I don't drink some coffee right away, I'm going to get heartburn so bad it'll kill me, he thought.

But all the cafés in town were still closed at that hour. He had no choice but to go home and make his own coffee. When he was done, he fired up a cigar and started wondering whether or not he should inform Montagnet of the trap he'd set for Don Filiberto. But he came to the conclusion that it would be best to talk to him afterwards and present him with a fait accompli. It was ninety-nine percent certain he wouldn't agree with the idea; he would say it was illegal.

But Teresi couldn't stay at home. He felt like he was suffocating. He glanced at his watch. An hour had gone by without him even noticing. He decided to leave, and as soon as he was out the door, he saw Stefano and Luigino at the far end of the street, returning home. He went back inside and, feeling his throat parched, drank a glass of water.

"It's done!" Stefano cried out loudly.

It was all Teresi could do not to start dancing.

"Did he give you the money?"

"No, Zio. He didn't have that much, which makes perfect sense. He said to come back later, around one, and he would have it for us."

"Tell me everything."

Stefano did the talking.

"When the priest went into the sacristy, we followed him and approached him just as he was taking off his vestments. As soon as he saw us he said: 'If this is going to take a while, please come back in an hour. I have to give last rites to a dying man.' I replied that it wouldn't take but a minute. 'Then go ahead and speak,' he said. But with a glance I let him understand that I didn't want to talk in front of the sacristan. He immediately got my message and ordered him to leave. As soon as it was just the three of us, I simply said: 'Rosalia killed herself.' He didn't say anything. Didn't ask when or where. Nothing. I got the impression he already knew. He leaned against the back of a chair with both hands, hung his head, and stayed that way for a minute, still without saying anything. I said I wanted to talk to him, but not in the sacristy, because other people might come in."

"And how did he react?"

"Want to know something strange, Zio? He didn't even ask what I wanted to talk to him about. He just nodded 'yes,' and walked towards the staircase, still keeping his head down."

"So he already knew! I'd bet the family jewels he already knew!" said Teresi.

"I was thinking the same thing," said Luigino.

"When we went upstairs, I told him that Rosalia had said what had happened first with Salamone and then with him. And when I finished, before I could even ask for the money, and without raising his head, he asked: 'How much?' I was so shocked I couldn't answer."

"So I answered for him," said Luigino. "'Two thousand,' I said."

"And what did he say?"

"He said simply: 'Come by later at one o'clock. I'll have the money for you. Now please leave by way of the sacristy door, and when you return, come back the same way.' And that was all. We went back down the stairs, but the priest stayed where he was."

Teresi sat there, looking pensive.

"What is it, Zio?"

"There's a problem that just occurred to me. From what you've just told me, it's clear the priest feels responsible for the girl's death. Caught by surprise, he agreed to give you the blackmail money. But can we trust him? If he talks about it with any other priests, they're sure to make him change his mind. And that's what could ruin us all. Or else he could change his mind on his own."

"And not give us the money?"

"He might even give it to you. But when I weigh in by writing an article about the whole thing in my weekly, he can still claim you guys made the whole thing up, that you tried to blackmail him, but he didn't give you one lira because he had nothing whatsoever to do with Rosalia's death. And if he finds out that you, Stefano, are not Rosalia's cousin but my nephew, and on top of that, that Luigino has never worked as a nurse at Camporeale hospital, then all three of us will end up in jail."

"So, what should we do?" asked Stefano.

"I'm going to tell the whole story to Montagnet. That should give us cover. Did you bring back the cheese and other stuff?"

Stefano slapped himself in the forehead.

"Damn! We completely forgot!"

*

Teresi dashed off to the carabinieri station, but Marshal Sciabbarrà told him the captain had just left for Camporeale, where he'd been summoned to report to the provincial commander, Colonel Chiaramonte.

"Do you know when he'll be back?"

"I can't really say."

"I'm sorry, but is it some sort of state secret?"

"No, sir, but the fact is that the colonel summoned him to a meeting in the early afternoon, and the captain decided to take advantage of the situation to drop in and see his family."

Teresi balked. Montagnet had a family? Seeing him always in uniform, with never a button out of place, elegant, impeccably groomed, inflexible, polite but aloof, Teresi had come to think of him as a kind of machine, not a man capable of the same feelings as other men.

"Is he married?"

"Yes, and he has two children. The boy is seven, the girl five. Is there anything I should tell him when he returns?"

"No, thank you, Marshal. I'll drop in again later."

*

So, what could he dream up to help the time pass? He went and paid a call on Giallonardo the notary. He wanted to know what he and his wife had decided about Rosalia. And if Giallonardo asked him why he was so interested, he would reply that he wanted to write an article about it. But there was no need to ask anything.

"My husband's not in," said Signura Romilda.

Her eyes were red. It was clear she'd been crying.

"When will he be back?"

"He's gone to Camporeale to bring Rosalia back here. Did you know she killed herself?"

Big tears began to roll down her cheeks.

"Yes, I was told."

"I'm sorry, but we were very fond of her, my husband and I. She was a poor orphan girl. We took her in when she wasn't even ten years old, poor little thing. Tomorrow, since the funeral can't be held in a church, I'm going to have Don Filiberto give his benediction outside the church of San Cono. He was so fond of Rosalia himself! He was always saying how devout she was! How powerful her faith!"

"And at what time will he give his blessing?"

"Tomorrow morning at nine."

"I'll be there."

He wouldn't have missed Don Filiberto Cusa's blessing for Rosalia for all the gold in the world.

*

While stepping out of the notary's house, he heard someone calling him. It was don Anselmo.

"How are we coming along?"

"On Totina's case?"

"Of course!"

Teresi decided to tell him a lie to keep him in check.

"It couldn't have been the husband of the sister of the wife of your overseer."

A complicated sentence, but he'd forgotten all those people's names, except for Totina's.

"Why not?"

"It's true he's eighty years old, as you say, but to look at him you'd think he's at least ninety. The guy can barely even breathe."

"But have you seen him in person?"

"Of course. With these two eyes. I always serve my clients honestly."

"But are you starting to get any ideas as to who it might have been?"

"I'm gathering information, don Anselmo."

"Well, I'm telling you: if and when you find out who did it, I want to be the first to know."

"But why are you so keen to know?"

"So I can shoot him."

"I'm sorry, but what has this got to do with you? You're not her father, husband or brother . . . "

"You're right! But I'll shoot him just the same! Come on! I've been raising the kid for twenty years, buying her things, giving her money without telling my wife, and the girl could never spare me even a caress or a little peck on the cheek . . . And now the first son of a bitch to come along suddenly gets her pregnant?"

*

Teresi made a plan. Go home, prepare a liter of chamomile tea, drink the whole thing, take a bath, change all his clothes because he was all sweaty, then go to the station at twelve-thirty and ask after Montagnet. If he happened to be in—which was impossible because the colonel had summoned him for an early afternoon meeting—he would tell him everything. If he wasn't, the only thing to do was to wait in front of the church, stop Stefano and Luigino when they arrived, and wait for Montagnet to return.

The lads weren't at home. Stefano's jacket with the mourning band on the sleeve was hanging from the coatrack. He would have to drop by to put it on. Beside it was the black tie. All at once, Teresi felt a chill run down his spine. *Matre santa*, what a terrible mistake they'd made that morning! Good thing it was still early and there were no people out on the street. Because anyone who knew Stefano, seeing the youth on the street, dressed in mourning, would surely have asked him who in his family had died! Teresi went into the lad's bedroom, took an overcoat from the armoire, and brought it into the entrance hall. Then he did what he'd decided to do, and as he was coming out of the bathroom, he heard Stefano return. He got dressed in a hurry. It was half past twelve.

"Where's Luigino?"

"He's waiting for me near the church."

"I'm going to the carabinieri station to see if Montagnet's there. And, listen: I want you to wear an overcoat. I put yours in the vestibule."

"Why?"

Teresi explained why.

"And if anyone asks why I'm wearing an overcoat?"

"Tell them you have the flu. Everyone's been getting the flu in this town, so why can't you?"

*

"No, there's been no news from the captain."

Teresi became discouraged. He was sure that Don Filiberto would give the money to Stefano, but also that as soon as he broke the story in his newssheet, the priest would claim that none of it was true, and that it was a scheme hatched up by the notorious anticlerical lawyer Matteo Teresi in cahoots with his nephew Stefano to drag the church's good name through the mud. His brain was telling him to dash over to San Cono and stop the two lads. But his instinct told him to let things take their course. His instinct won out.

He raced back home, got undressed down to his underpants, and lay down in bed with his head under the pillow.

Then, a little while later, he heard the front door of the house open and close. He pulled his head out from under the pillow. He could hear the two youths in the kitchen, but they weren't talking or laughing. What had happened?

He went downstairs dressed just as he was. Stefano hadn't even taken his coat off and was sitting in a chair, drinking a glass of water. He looked pale. Luigino was also sitting down, his head in his hands.

Neither of the two seemed to have noticed Teresi.

"So what happened?"

They said nothing.

"Jesus Christ, would you tell me what happened?" said Teresi, raising his voice.

"The priest hanged himself," said Luigino.

Teresi felt the ground give out from under his feet. The trap he'd laid for the priest had worked all too well. Damn the moment he got that brilliant idea!

"Did anyone see you go in or come out?"

"No."

"Tell me about it."

"We entered by way of the sacristy door, which was open," said Luigino. "We went upstairs, and there he was, in the first room. Hanging from the ceiling. It was . . . ghastly. There was an envelope on the table."

"Did you take it?"

"Yes. And I put it in Stefano's pocket. I had to literally drag him out of there. He was in shock and couldn't move."

Teresi looked over at his nephew. The lad's eyes were open wide and staring into space. He went up to him, stuck his hand in the youth's pocket, took the envelope out, and opened it.

You won't get the money you wanted, because I was unable to find anyone to lend me such a sum. In exchange, I give you my confession. I abused Rosalia Pampina, my parishioner, for a long time, and in unnatural ways, making her believe that what we were doing were secret practices to ward off temptation and to allow her to remain pure until marriage. But the evening she came to confess about having been raped by Salamone the brigand, I don't know what got into me. What Rosalia said isn't exactly correct—that is, that the penance is like the sin. In fact, the penance was worse than the sin. You can sell this letter of mine to a newspaper, if you like. They will surely pay you more than what you asked of me.

This was followed only by the man's signature.

"Do me a favor," Teresi said to Luigino. "Go and look for Dr. Palumbo and bring him back here. I'm getting worried about Stefano."

Chapter XI
An Inconvenient Death

It was the sacristan, Virgilio Bellofiore, who discovered the body of Patre Filiberto, whereupon the whole town did a repeat—that is, descended into a pandemonium almost exactly like the one unleashed on the day of don Anselmo's cholera.

Spooked as he was, the sacristan, dashing out of the house, missed a step and rolled all the way down the staircase, smashing his nose. Then, picking himself up, he went out into the street with his face covered in blood and shouting desperately:

"Don Filiberto killed himself!"

These words were quickly passed from mouth to mouth by hundreds of people. Those in the street repeated them to those at their windows, while those at their windows shouted them at those on their balconies, and those on their balconies yelled them at those on their terraces, while those on their terraces shouted them in turn at the wind, and the wind soon carried the news out into the countryside around Palizzolo.

What happened next was that whoever was eating stopped eating; whoever was sleeping woke up; whoever was breastfeeding laid the crying baby down; whoever was working in the vegetable garden set the hoe aside; whoever was dying managed to stave off death; and whoever was making love stopped in the very midst.

And all those who could do so ran towards the church of San Cono, filled up Piazza Garibaldi, and clogged the nearby streets.

"Is it really true he killed himself?"

"Apparently."

"But is it true or not true?"

"It's true."

"And how did he kill himself?"

"With rat poison."

"He shot himself."

"He threw himself off the balcony."

"He inhaled the smoke from the bedwarmer."

"He hung himself from a ceiling rafter."

"He stabbed himself in the heart."

"But why?"

"He'd gone crazy."

"He was a gambler. He'd lost a lot of money playing *zicchinetta.*"

"Come on! The man had never seen a playing card in his life!"

"He was sick."

"He had debts."

"He'd quarreled with the bishop."

"He didn't believe in God anymore."

"Did he leave any note?"

"Nothing."

"What do you mean, nothing? When someone kills himself, he always leaves a note saying why!"

"This whole thing is very strange!"

"Extremely strange!"

"Maybe he wrote to the bishop."

"Maybe he did write a letter, which they then destroyed."

"Who?"

"I dunno! The sacristan, for one."

"And why would he destroy it?"

"Maybe it said some compromising things."

"Bah!"

"Now I'm having my doubts."

"And what if he didn't kill himself?"

"What do you mean, didn't kill himself?"

"I mean, what if he was killed and then they made it look like he killed himself?"

"And why was the sacristan's face all bloody?"

"Maybe he caught the killers in the act."

"Then why was he yelling that the priest had killed himself?"

"'Cause they threatened him. They would've killed him too, if he didn't say what he did."

"That's bullshit!"

"Who would have wanted to kill Don Filiberto?"

"He didn't have any enemies."

"All he ever did was good."

"He helped everybody."

"He always had a good thing to say about everyone."

"He would take from himself to give to others!"

"He was an honest man! A great man!"

"A great man? He was a saint!"

"A saint! A saint! A saint!"

Growing more and more excited, the throng began to move forward, perhaps to go into the church to get a glimpse of the saint's mortal remains, or else to give vent to all the agitation they'd been subjected to of late, from the cholera scare to the arrest of Marquis Cammarata.

"Saint! Saint! Saint!"

"Let's break down the door of the church!"

"Let's grab the saint for ourselves!"

"We'll have a procession and march him through town!"

The six carabinieri who'd formed a cordon in front of the church started backpedaling.

Marshal Sciabbarrà felt lost. If the crazed mob actually did manage to get their hands on the corpse, they would surely tear it immediately to pieces, each trying to get his own personal relic.

Without thinking twice, he cocked his revolver and fired twice in the air. Everyone fled. Everyone, that is, except eighty-year-old *ragioniere* Michele Orlando, who lay on the ground in the middle of the piazza, cut down by a heart attack.

*

The sacristan, meanwhile, had raced over to the nearest church, which was San Giovanni. The main door was half closed. Dashing in, he nearly crashed into Don Alessio Terranova, the parish priest, who was just coming out to close up.

"Don Filiberto killed himself!"

Don Alessio froze with his left foot in midair, unable to complete his step.

"What the hell are you saying?"

"He killed himself! Hung himself from a rafter! I saw him with my own eyes!"

Don Alessio set his left foot down.

"Did he leave any kind of written message?"

"I didn't see anything! But it really spooked me!"

"Go and wash your face!"

These words took the sacristan by surprise. He didn't understand.

"What did you say?"

"Wash your face. It's all covered with blood."

"I'll go into the sacristy."

"No, don't waste any time. Wash it right here, with the holy water in the baptismal font. Then go and tell Patre Raccuglia, Patre Scurria, Patre Samonà, Patre Marrafà, and Patre Pintacuda."

"You forgot Patre Dalli Cardillo."

"No, I didn't forget him. There's no need to go and talk to Patre Dalli Cardillo. But you must tell all the others to meet here, in no more than fifteen minutes."

*

"Listen, Marshal, they told us at the courthouse that no judges are available at the moment."

"What do they mean 'at the moment'?" Marshal Sciabbarrà asked his colleague at the other end of the telephone line.

"They mean that before tomorrow no magistrate from Camporeale can come to Palizzolo."

"So I'm supposed to leave the priest dangling from the rafter until tomorrow?"

"I have an idea. Cut the rope he's hanging from, and later, when they ask you about it, tell them you did it because you thought the priest was still alive."

"All right, but then what am I going to do with the corpse?"

"Have somebody fashion a catafalque from the bedclothes and posts, then put it out on display in the church."

"What the hell are you saying?"

"Why, what's wrong with that?"

"If the bishop comes and sees it, he'll break my neck! Don Filiberto is excommunicated, since he killed himself!"

"You're right. Wait, let me ask the captain."

Three minutes went by during which Marshal Scibbarrà damned his soul by dint of curses.

"Sciabbarrà? The captain wants to know if there are any chests in the sacristy."

"Yes, there are two or three."

"Wait just a second."

The marshal had all time he needed to utter every curse he knew.

"Sciabbarrà? The captain says you should bring the body down into the sacristy and put it temporarily in one of the chests."

"What about afterwards?"

"We'll see about what to do afterwards. And don't let anyone into the sacristy."

*

His Most Reverend Excellency Egilberto Martire, bishop of Camporeale, normally took a half-hour nap after eating. That day, before dozing off, he'd given an order to his staff.

"You mustn't wake me for any reason! I don't want to be bothered for anything, even if you start hearing the goddamn trumpets of the Apocalypse!"

Therefore his secretary, Don Marcantonio Panza, solved the problem by calling his second secretary, Don Costantino Perna.

"Listen, Don Costantino, I just now got a phone call from the mayor of Palizzolo. Apparently the priest of San Cono parish, Don Filiberto Cusa, has killed himself."

"Killed himself?! *O Madonna benedetta!* How very strange! Are they sure?"

"That's exactly why I've decided to go straight to Palizzolo myself. I'd like to confirm things in person. I'll inform His Excellency by telephone. And when he wakes up, you must tell him everything, but with the utmost caution."

*

With the help of two carabinieri and Lance Corporal Magnacavallo, Marshal Scibbarrà did what the captain had said and, just to be sure, not only covered the chest with the priestly vestments he'd found inside, but placed four heavy bronze candelabra on top as well. Then he left the lance corporal and carabinieri on guard outside the sacristy door, to prevent anyone from going in, and headed back to the station.

Half an hour later, the lance corporal found six priests he already knew standing before him.

"We've come to bless the mortal remains of our unfortunate brother," said a sorrowful Don Alessio Terranova, opening his cloak so the guard could see the aspergillum and basin he'd brought.

Lance Corporal Magnacavallo broke out in a cold sweat. Now what was he going to tell these priests? Could he possibly tell them they'd put the body inside a chest? Then he had an idea.

"He's no longer here."

"Then were is he?"

"He was taken . . . to the station."

"And where is the train headed?"

"No, sir, I meant to our station, the carabinieri compound. But you can't see him."

"And why not?"

"I have no idea. By order of the judge in Camporeale."

The six priests stepped back and started conferring amongst themselves.

Then Patre Pinta went back on the attack.

"We need to go into the home of our poor late brother."

"It's not possible. I have orders to—"

"You can't treat us this way!" screeched Patre Marrafà.

"We're not common thieves! We're priests!" shouted Patre Scurria.

"And you, corporal, you know us perfectly well! You know who we are!" yelled Patre Raccuglia.

The windows of the house opposite opened, and some faces appeared.

All they needed was more chaos.

"All right, go on in," said the lance corporal.

*

Five minutes after the social club opened for the afternoon, as scheduled, at three o'clock, the salon was already mobbed. Giallonardo the notary was receiving the members' condolences as if he had been a relative of Don Filiberto.

"But, the last time you spoke to him, Signor Giallonardo, how did he seem?" asked don Liborio Spartà, the president.

"Well, the last time . . . he started crying."

"Crying? Don Filiberto seemed like such a strong man . . . "

"Thirty-nine years old, poor man!" said Colonel Petrosillo.

"What's that got to do with anything? Thirty-nine years old or forty, the fact is the man was crying!" don Anselmo Buttafava retorted.

"Gentlemen, I would like to clarify that it was a rather unusual occasion," Giallonardo resumed speaking.

"And what was that? Can you tell us?" asked Professor Malatesta.

"It's no secret. When my housekeeper Rosalia killed herself the day before yesterday by throwing herself out a fourth-floor window at Camporeale hospital . . . "

"Your housekeeper killed herself?" asked don Stapino Vassallo.

"That's what I just said, isn't it?"

"Yes, but why did she do it?"

"Nobody knows."

"But would you just let him finish speaking without interruption?" said don Serafino Labianca.

" . . . I went to see Don Filiberto," the notary resumed, "and I asked him if he would be so kind as to give the dead girl benediction. He said yes, and then started crying."

"But the question remains: Why did he start crying?" asked don Serafino.

"Rosalia was a parishioner of his."

"But, my good notary, if a priest cried over every one of his parishioners who died, he'd go blind in a month, believe me."

"But he was particularly fond of Rosalia!"

"Oh, was he?"

"Yes, he was! He cared a great deal for her and admired her. He always used to talk about what a good girl she was, so respectful and devout . . . He would often keep her a long time in the sacristy . . . "

"In the sacristy?" President Spartà repeated.

"Yes, what's so strange about that? Isn't catechism taught in the sacristy?"

"Bah!" said don Serafino.

"And what is 'bah' supposed to mean?"

"It means, Mr. Notary, that two plus two makes four!"

"I agree!" Colonel Petrosillo chimed in.

"But you agree with what, exactly?"

"Mr. Notary, it's quite simple: Don Filiberto killed himself because he was in love with Rosalia," don Serafino said bluntly.

"And Rosalia killed herself because she herself was in love with Don Filiberto!" the colonel said, smiling. "An impossible love!"

"Colonel, you know as well as anybody that there's no such thing as an impossible love," said don Anselmo.

The colonel took umbrage.

"And just what are you insinuating?"

"I'm merely saying that if they loved each other so much, the priest could easily have taken his frock off and hooked up with the girl. It certainly wouldn't have been the first time, nor the last!"

"Ah, the flesh is weak!" the colonel sighed.

"And yet," said President Spartà, "we mustn't necessarily

dismiss the possibility that they were in love. Was Rosalia by any chance pregnant?"

"Oh, stop speaking twaddle!" the notary snapped. "Patre Filibeto was a saint, just as people say."

"Sainthood and earthly love can easily coexist," the colonel proclaimed.

*

An hour later another meeting was held at the castle of Duke Ruggero d'Altomonte. Except for Marquis Cammarata, all the local nobles were there.

"What's this about the priest of San Cono parish?" asked Baron Roccamena.

"Just now at the club, people were saying that he killed himself because he was in love with a girl and got her pregnant," Baron Piscopo replied.

Hearing the word *pregnant*, Baron Lo Mascolo turned pale.

"Why did you summon us here?" the Baron Roccamena asked Marquis Spinotta.

"Because the other day you asked me to telephone my cousin, Duke Simone Loreto di San Loreto."

"And did you?"

"Of course I did."

"And what did the duke say?"

"He said he would look into the matter immediately. And indeed he called me back just two hours ago."

He paused for effect. And amidst the silence one could hear the hoarse voice of Duke Ruggero in the background saying:

"It's all the fault of the French Revolution!"

"And so?" Baron Roccamena pressed the marquis.

"He told me the provincial commander of the carabinieri, Colonel Chiaramonte, has summoned Captain Montagnet to tell him he must return immediately to Camporeale. So now we've finally got him out of our hair, once and for all," the marquis concluded, to the general exultation of all present.

*

They didn't know, however, that Captain Montagnet was in fact on his way back to Palizzolo.

What had happened was that around three o'clock that afternoon, as the captain was waiting for the colonel's call, another phone call came in, this one from Marshal Sciabbarrà.

"Ciaramiddaro, I urgently need to speak with Captain Montagnet."

"It's not possible. He's in the colonel's antechamber."

"Is the adjutant Sinibaldi there?"

"Yes, I'll put him on."

"Hello, Sciabbarrà, how are you?"

"Major, sir, Captain Montagnet at the moment is in the colonel's anteroom. I need to inform him that the situation here in Palizzolo is becoming difficult again."

"How?"

"Don Filiberto Cusa, a parish priest, has killed himself."

"So what?"

"There've been clashes between some of Don Filiberto's parishioners and people from other churches in town. The latter group claims that Don Filiberto seduced a young female parishioner of his, and Don Filiberto's faithful are up in arms. So far we've had two stabbings. So far."

"Do you fear further complications?"

"As surely as death."

"All right, thanks."

The adjutant knew already what the colonel was going to say to Montagnet, and so, instead of speaking with the captain, he thought it best to mention the phone call directly to Commander Chiaramonte.

As a result, when he was finally received, the captain was told by the colonel that, although the order had come from "higher up" for him to return at once to Camporeale, the situation had at Palizzolo had changed again, due to the priest's suicide, and so he was granted a week's extension.

*

Before leaving for Palizzolo, Don Marcantonio Panza had obtained from the courts of Camporeale a document written and signed by President Onorio Labarbera, which went as follows: "Don Marcantonio Panza, secretary to His Excellency Egilberto Martire, bishop of Camporeale, is hereby granted full access to the Church of San Cono and adjacent rooms (sacristy, priory, etc.), to allow him to catalogue all objects belonging to the late Don Filiberto Cusa and arrange for the shipment of said objects to the priest's family."

Upon arrival, Don Marcantonio presented the document to Lance Corporal Magnacavallo, who let him in. But less than five minutes later, the guard heard the envoy call him from inside the sacristy.

"Corporal, please come here for a moment."

The young man shuddered. The envoy had probably discovered the corpse inside the chest! But that wasn't the case. The chest was just as they'd left it.

"Would you please follow me?" said the priest.

Following behind him, he climbed the wooden staircase and entered the room where Don Filiberto had hanged himself.

The lance corporal froze in the doorway. It looked as if a cyclone had torn through the room. Drawers, cabinets, glass cupboards, and everything else had been opened, and all their contents thrown onto the floor.

"Go and have a look in the other room and the bedroom."

In the second room, a desk had been overturned, its feet now in the air, drawers open and totally empty. The parish's registers, papers, and documents were all gone. There wasn't a single sheet of paper to be seen anywhere.

In the bedroom, even the mattresses had been torn open and gutted.

"What reason could your people have possibly had to do all this?" asked Don Marcantonio.

"My people?!" the corporal began, trembling with rage.

"Who, then?"

"It was those other priests, whom I, like an idiot, was stupid enough to let in here!"

They went back into the first room.

"Are you sure about what you just said?"

"And what was that?"

"That it was the other parish priests who took all the papers away."

"Yes, sir, I'm absolutely certain. And I'm going to report it immediately to the marshal."

Don Marcantonio looked up and cut the remaining rope still dangling from the rafter.

"Where have you taken him?"

"To the carabinieri station."

"You were right to do so. The body won't be allowed into a church, and therefore cannot have a funeral mass said for it, and cannot be buried in consecrated land."

The lance corporal made such a bewildered face that Don Marcantonio couldn't help but notice. He threw up his hands.

"Are you sorry? There are rules, however, and they must be respected. Suicide is an act against God."

"And what about Count Mortillaro?"

The lance corporal bit his lip. The question had just slipped out. Two years earlier, Count Mortillaro had shot himself in the head. He'd been given a solemn funeral and buried in the family vault.

"That was a very different case," Don Marcantonio said brusquely.

Want to bet, thought Lance Corporal Magnacavallo, that they would end up having to take the dead priest to the station after all, and hide him in the closet?

*

Matteo Teresi was at home, thinking about the article he had to write that night, when a carabiniere came to tell him that the captain wanted urgently to see him.

"What's your part in all this confusion?" was Montagnet's first question.

"Well, Captain, you'd suggested that I write an insinuating article, but in the meantime I was lucky enough to run into a witness, someone who'd seen Rosalia come out of the church after eight o'clock, and so . . . "

He told him everything, even about the blackmailing charade. As he was talking, the captain's face turned darker and darker.

"I ought to arrest you for disturbing the peace. And this time I wouldn't be wrong, as I was with Dr. Bellanca. However, I believe you're right."

"About what?"

"Just after the news of the suicide began to spread, six parish priests dashed over to Don Filiberto's residence, turned the place upside down, and took away all the papers they found there. Who knows what they were looking for."

"They were looking for this," said Teresi, taking out the letter written by Don Cusa and setting it down on the desk.

Chapter XII
Four Articles, Two Monologues, and One Dialogue

Two days after the the death of the parish priest of San Cono, Matteo Teresi published in his newssheet an article he'd written after coming to an agreement with Captain Montagnet, the title of which was "The Penance Is Like the Sin," with, as subhead, "The Truth on the Suicide of Don Cusa."

It went as follows:

There have been many diverse and conflicting rumors circulating among the population of Palizzolo (and among those of the nearby towns, even in Camporeale, the provincial capital) concerning the reasons that may have driven thirty-nine-year-old Don Filiberto Cusa, priest of the local parish of San Cono, to commit the tragic act that has created such a stir.

We are now able to reveal to our readers the truth of the matter, thanks to a handwritten letter from Don Cusa himself, drafted just minutes before he took his life. We were able to read this letter before turning it dutifully over, as we have done, to the proper authorities at the Court of Camporeale.

In just a few brief lines, Don Cusa confesses to having deceived, over a certain period of time, a naïve young member of his parish, Rosalia P., subjecting her to such unnatural practices as masturbation and fellatio, which he presented as magical religious rites designed to protect the young woman from the temptations of the flesh. We will not dwell here on the tawdry details.

On the day when a rumor spread throughout Palizzolo

that cholera had descended upon the town, the young woman fled to the countryside with two female friends. But during the night the three women had the misfortune of crossing paths with the noted brigand Salamone, who set upon Rosalia with particular ferocity and at great length, keeping her prisoner for an entire night and the following morning, until he was captured by the valorous Lieutenant of the Royal Carabinieri Rodolfo Villasevaglios.

Returning that same day to her place of residence, where she worked as a housemaid (but was treated like a daughter), the young woman asked that evening for permission to go to the church of San Cono, where Vespers had just rung, so she could meet with Don Filiberto. After hearing the girl's confession, and her description of what the brigand had put her through, the priest, blinded by his passions, convinced her to come with him into the sacristy and then to his apartment upstairs, where he subjected her to a series of "penances" that were in no way any less cruel and ferocious than the turpitudes of the brigand Salamone. When she came back out through the sacristy door an hour and a half later, shaken and upset, Rosalia was aided and escorted back to her residence by an acquaintance. As of that moment, she refused to speak, eat, or drink.

Dr. Palumbo of Palizzolo was promptly summoned to examine the young woman, and after administering first aid decided it was best for her to be admitted to Camporeale hospital.

After verifying the terrible abuse the girl had undergone and assessing her mental state, the hospital's chief physician dutifully reported the matter to the Royal Carabinieri. The investigation was assigned to Captain Eugenio Montagnet, who noticed, after questioning Don Filiberto, that the priest's claim to have seen Rosalia leave the church right after her confession was inconsistent with the time of the girl's return home, at 8:30 P.M., as reported by her patroness. The testimony of the acquaintance who had come to her aid instead indicated that Rosalia had remained inside the church until that time—a period lasting about an hour and a half. This was as far as the investigation had got at the moment when the unhappy Rosalia unexpectedly took her own life, throwing herself out of a fourth-floor window of the hospital where she was staying. The previous evening, however, she had in fact resumed talking, only to utter, in the presence of the doctor and the nurse, this terrible statement: "The penance is like the sin."

The horrific meaning of these words will surely not escape our readers' comprehension.

At this point Captain Montagnet resorted to a strategy to corner the priest. Finding himself with no way out, and gripped by remorse, the priest decided to take his own life.

Don Filiberto's mortal remains have been reclaimed by his brother, Orazio, who lives in Quattrocastagni.

Such, then, are the facts concerning this suicide.

There is, however, another episode, in itself quite alarming, which has come to our attention. Shortly after the news of Don Filiberto's tragic death began to spread, the priests of the other parishes of Palizzolo (namely, Don Alessio Terranova, Don Eriberto Raccuglia, Don Alighiero Scurria, Don Libertino Samonà, Don Angelo Marrafà, and Don Ernesto Pintacuda), with the sole exception of Don Mariano Dalli Cardillo, priest of the parish of the SS. Crocefisso, presented themselves to the lance corporal of the Royal Carabinieri assigned to guard the door to the sacristy, and asked to be granted entry to Don Filiberto's apartment in order to bless his mortal remains. Upon being categorically refused, the priests began to raise such a row that the carabiniere, to avoid further tension, let them in. The six priests spent a good deal of time, unsupervised, in the apartment, and then left. Shortly thereafter, Don Marcantonio Panza, secretary of His Most Reverend Excellency, Bishop Egilberto Martire, equipped with a lawful authorization from the Court of Camporeale, appeared before the same lance corporal. Upon going upstairs into the late Don Filiberto Cusa's apartment, however, he immediately summoned the corporal into the residence and showed him that the apartment had been turned upside down, apparently as the result of a frantic search, and that every document, including private letters, receipts and the like, had been removed, apparently by the other priests.

Upon learning that the secretary of His Excellency the Bishop was in Palizzolo, Captain Montagnet held a meeting with the emissary in the course of which he informed him that he intended to request the authorization of the Court of Camporeale to institute legal action against the six priests for theft of materials placed under restriction by the authority of the judiciary.

We will keep our readers informed as this case develops.

A few questions remain, however. What were the reverend fathers looking for in their confrère's home? Were they perhaps afraid that Don Filiberto had left behind some compromising materials? And, if so, compromising for whom?

*

"What a fine-looking bunch you are, all six of you! Young, healthy, strong, vivacious, full of fire, initiative, and will to live . . . Real soldiers of Christ! Good for you! The problem is you haven't got a goddamn thing in your heads! Now, I've summoned you here to tell you something really quick. But let me preface by saying that, though my family name may be Martire, I have no desire whatsoever to become a martyr for your sakes. Got that? I have to tell you that this morning I got a phone call from the Presiding Judge of the Court, the eminent Commendatore Onorio Laberbera, who is such a pants-shitting coward[4] . . . Anyway, he says to me: You must understand my position, your excellency, I cannot ignore Captain Montagnet's request . . . I have no choice but to grant him authorization and so on and so forth . . . And so, in the end I said to him: Who's asking you for anything? The law must take its course, says he. So I says: Then let it take this famous course! Do you understand what that means? If they have to arrest you, they're gonna arrest you. All of you. An' I won't lift a finger. I don't want any trouble. You break something, you fix it yourselves. What need was there for all six of you to trudge over there to that wretch's home? One of you woulda been enough. You have a look at whatever there is to look at, you take whatever there is to take, and you leave everything just the way it was. Nice and neat. But since you're all stupid young shits, you broke all the eggs. You even took the parish registers! What the hell were you looking for? Wait! Don't tell me! Don't tell me! I don't want to know! That's your goddamn business, not mine. You've all got pumpkins for heads! For now, all I'm gonna say is that, starting tomorrow, you'll all be replaced by other priests from the diocese, at least until this whole story blows over. Only Don Dalli Cardillo will keep his position. No! Not a word! Cuz if you start talking I'll kick your asses from here to kingdom come! Now, get the hell outta here, all of you! Hop to it!"

[4] In the original text, the Bishop, who speaks in Roman dialect, says that Labarbera "*è tanto, ma tanto scacarcione*," a phrase clearly echoing a line by 19th-century *romanesco* (Roman dialect) poet Giuseppe Gioacchino Belli, a man of severely anticlerical sentiment. Writing of Pope Gregory XVI, Belli writes: "*Povero frate! è ttanto scacarcione / Che ssi una rondinella passa e fischia / La pijja pe 'na palle de cannone.*" ("Poor brother! He's such a pants-shitting coward / That if a swallow passes and tweets / He takes it for a cannonball.")

*

Two days after the first article, Teresi wrote another, which he published in a special one-page edition of his newsheet.

The article was entitled *Let's Venture an Hypothesis.*

It went as follows:

We know from an unimpeachable source that His Excellency, the Most Reverend Egilberto Martire, bishop of Camporeale, when faced with the request to institute legal proceedings against six Palizzolo parish priests for removing and absconding with documents under legal sequester (a crime calling for the arrest of the culprit(s)), declared his willingness not to obstruct the pursuit of Justice, adding that he has relieved the six priests temporarily of their duties, replacing them with six other priests from the diocese who will lead their respective parishes. Such a gesture once again underscores the great wisdom of His Excellency the Bishop, which we have seen at work on other occasions of considerably less gravity.

What the bishop refrained from doing was instead done by the Camporeale correspondent for the main newspaper of Sicily, who fiercely defended the actions of the six priests, asserting that it was fully within their rights to remove the parish documents so that the activities of the parish might not suffer any interruptions or slowdowns due to the tragic death of their spiritual leader.

But, if this were really the case, what need was there to deceive the carabiniere on duty? Perhaps all the six priests had to do was to say this, in order to persuade the officer of the law, who then would no doubt have gladly accompanied them into the late Don Filiberto's apartment and requested and obtained a proper receipt for any registers taken away.

Or else they could have addressed the Court (as indeed the bishop's secretary, Don Marcantonio Panza, had done) to request and obtain the necessary authorization.

But the six priests did not proceed in this fashion, my distinguished colleague in journalism. They didn't want any prying eyes to see them as they ransacked the apartment.

And even if they now are anxiously declaring that they have turned over to Captain Montagnet everything they spirited away, hidden under their robes, what guarantee do we have that this is true? And if it happens that they have not returned absolutely everything, what might these priests have wanted to keep for themselves?

In my capacity as a journalist, I have conducted a modest investigation that has yielded an interesting result. I requested from the Court, and obtained, permission to enter the late priest's domicile. Nothing had been touched since the ransacking. The apartment was still in a state of indescribable disarray, such as the the six priests left it after their visit. In one corner of the dining room stood a painter's easel, beside a small overturned table that had once held the paints and brushes now scattered across the floor. Don Filiberto was indeed known as an amateur painter, and a number of paintings of religious subjects were hanging on the walls of his apartment.

This triggered a suspicion in me. During a conversation with the sacristan, Virgilio Bellofiore, I found my suspicion confirmed. Signor Bellofiore told me that Don Filiberto used to carry around some notebook pages on which he would sketch in pencil the things that struck him most over the course of the day, and he usually would store these drawings in the drawers of his desk. The priest's daytime housekeeper, Signora Amelia Putifarro, also confirmed this fact.

Let's venture a hypothesis: Is it possible that the six priests were not looking for documents at all, but for compromising drawings? Perhaps the drawings he kept in his drawers were not compromising, but Don Filiberto may have hidden other more salacious ones in more secret places in his apartment. This would explain the need to search everywhere in his home.

I have dutifully brought this hypothesis to the attention of Captain Montagnet. So far, however, the captain has not deemed it necessary to arrest the six priests.

It is therefore with some regret that I must conclude that our hypothesis is henceforth almost certainly destined to remain nothing more than that, since by now it is unlikely any trace remains of such drawings.

*

"This is the first time I've come to confess to you, Patre Dalli Cardillo. I used to always go to the Church of the Heart of Jesus and confess to Patre Alighiero Scurria, but I don't want to do that anymore. I need more than just an absolution, Don Mariano. I need some advice. I haven't been able to sleep for the past few nights, ever since I read in the paper that Rosalia Pampina killed herself over what Don Filiberto did to her. I met Rosalia a little more than a couple of months ago, when the priests took us out to the Benedictine convent, which was empty, for a day of retreat and spiritual exercises. There was me, Rosalia, Baron Lo Mascolo's daughter Antonietta, the daughter of don Anselmo Buttafava's overseer, Totina, Marquis Cammarata's daughter Paolina, Lorenza Spagna, who was the youngest of all of us, since she's only fifteen and a half, and Filippa Lanza, who's the daughter of the bank president. There was one of us from each church, chosen by her own parish priest. I'm a widow, and I'm twenty-four years old and have no children. Ever since my husband died I've really been missing him and suffering a lot, and I confessed to Patre Scurria that

I often have naughty dreams, and sometimes I touch myself . . . And he told me he would do an exorcism on me, which we would have to renew once a week, and that would keep me pure.

"He had me look at an ancient book, all written in Latin, with pictures. One showing a devil doing it with a naked lady . . . An' he explained that when I touch myself, though I think I'm alone, the devil is always there, taking me like he's taking the woman in the picture. An' he also said that it wasn't the thing itself that was a sin, but the intention you do it with. An' if the intention is right, it can change the sin into a purification. Anyway, he convinced me. An' then there was the day of spiritual exercises. With all the consecrated wine we were drinking, we all got drunk. An' two hours later we were all naked, men and women alike . . . An' as soon as one priest was finished with one of us, another would pick her up . . . As for Rosalia, Patre Filiberto ordered everyone to preserve her virginity, but for all the rest of us . . . Anyway, so they got me pregnant, and a few other girls, too, I'm sure. An' it's true what the newspaper says: Don Filiberto was fucking and drawing pictures. I'm so mad, Don Mariano, so mad and desperate. They took advantage of me and my trust, my honesty, and my faith most of all. Now I've got a baby in my belly an' I don't even know who the father is, 'cause they all had a turn with me. I read in the paper today about the drawings . . . An' I had an idea: I'm gonna go to the Carabinieri an' tell 'em everything, I thought. An' if they don't believe me, I'll tell 'em Patre Scurria's got a red spot on his bum, Patre Raccuglia's got a great big wart under his belly button, and Don Libertino—Wha', Father? That's enough, you say? Okay, I'll stop. What are you doing, Don Mariano, are you crying? I know how you feel! You're the only real priest in this town! But what do you think I should do? Should I go to the Carabinieri?"

*

Just two days after our special edition, we find ourselves again faced with the need to publish another, to inform our readers of the incredible developments emerging in Carabinieri Captain Montagnet's investigation into the actions of the six Palizzolo priests, who are, by name: Don Alessio Terranova, Don Eriberto Raccuglia, Don Alighiero Scurria, Don Libertino Samonà, Don Angelo Marrafà, and Don Ernesto Pintacuda.

They were all arrested yesterday evening, not only for removing documents under sequester and absconding with them, but for far more serious charges, including the sexual assault and rape of seven women belonging to their parishes (including no fewer than three minors!), whom they morally subjugated, through dubious "purification rites," into consenting to their lusts. Indeed, so subjugated have these women been, that those who are now pregnant continue to claim that the infants in their wombs are the work of the Holy Spirit or the will of God. In short, our fine parish priests had created a veritable sect—which we'll here call, ironically, "The Sect of Angels"—in which they passed off patently obscene acts as mystical religious rites.

This all reached an apex of depravity a little more than two months ago in a group orgy (which the priests called a "spiritual retreat"), lasting an entire day, at the Benedictine Convent, which was reopened for the occasion. The profusion of spirituality yielded concrete results: four of the seven women participating in the retreat came away pregnant. And thus these Fathers became fathers! Except that none of the four women (including two of the three minors) will ever know which priest sired her child, since they were all subjected to abuse by more than one priest that day.

Upon hearing the news that the six priests had admitted

guilt to all of the crimes with which they were charged, and further explained that they had ransacked Don Cusa's apartment to remove some sketches bearing witness to their orgy—as I had earlier conjectured—His Excellency the Bishop of Camporeale suspended them of their religious duties "a divinis."

What does my eminent journalistic colleague, who defended them with sword drawn in Sicily's most important newspaper, think of all this?

On the matter of these drawings, a clarification is in order.

The priests did not find them in their search, despite turning the apartment upside down looking for them.

They were located by Captain Montagnet in a hollow carved into the hearth of Don Filiberto's kitchen and then covered up with an earthenware tile.

And in the detailed, meticulous rendering of the faces, they drawings serve as incontrovertible evidence of the priests' guilt.

Matteo Teresi then published a fourth article on the matter in the regular edition, rather than a special one, of his newssheet, which went by the name of *The Battle*.

By this point there was no longer anything so special about any of it. Or so, at least, he believed.

On more than one occasion, I, and those associated with this journal, have been accused of being instigators, subversives, and prejudiced anticlerics.

I would like to point out to our readers that on the occasion of the ridiculous cholera outbreak, which proved nonexistent, I was fingered by seven of the eight pulpits of Palizzolo as the sole person responsible for the supposed epidemic.

I was guilty, said the priests, of having brought the wrath of God upon our town.

There was even a priest who organized and personally led

an attack upon my home, which was fortunately aborted. Yet their declared purpose was to kill the devil, whom I had supposedly come to incarnate.

Even now, after the priests have fully admitted to committing their odious acts, malicious rumors about me persist, insinuating that the whole affair was an underhanded maneuver motivated by my insatiable hatred of the Church!

And that is not all.

There is even one person who has dared write that an "accursèd alliance" [sic!] has been created in Palizzolo between a freebooting lawyer who disparages all that is sacred in his quest for notoriety and an officer of the Carabinieri who has been granted too much freedom of action and has exploited this fact to take measures well beyond the limits of his legitimate duties.

In other words, Captain Montagnet and the present writer are engaged in an iniquitous conspiracy.

Another has claimed that the captain's manner of proceeding has actually been dictated by the disdain the Piedmontese feel towards Sicilians.

Pure humbug.

What is, in essence, being absurdly and blindly maintained in such accusations is the premise that the lawyer and the officer of the law are in cahoots to deliver a mortal blow to the summit of our social system, as represented by the Aristocracy and the Church.

The supposed attack upon the Aristocracy—let us not forget—is represented by the "unjust" (!) arrest of the Marquis Cammarata and the public outcry said to have been purposely created by the very manner in which the marquis was arrested.

What the rumormongers omit from their story, however, is that the clamor arose directly from the actions of the marquis's own family, who began shouting obscenities at the carabinieri carrying out the arrest, and from the behavior of Marquis

Cammarata himself, who, though handcuffed, managed, in a surge of bestial rage, to bite the ear of the carabiniere marshal and draw blood.

And they omitted one scarcely negligible detail above all, which is that the marquis himself has confessed to the crime of attempted murder with the complicity of a noted local Mafia chieftain still at large.

Captain Montagnet has therefore done nothing more than fulfill his duty. Conscientiously, I would add. With little fear of anyone. As is the custom for those who have the honor of belonging to the Royal Order of Carabinieri.

As for the accusation of an attack on the Church, let us say, once and for all: Enough!

To this end, I present below, verbatim, the indignant words an illustrious priest, Don Luigi Sturzo, has written for Il Sole del Mezzogiorno, *the newspaper published in Palermo, in its July 15–16, 1901, edition:*

Readers may not know that in the town of Palizzolo, there exists a sect, derisively said to be "of angels," composed of a number of degenerate priests unworthy of their holy ministry, unworthy even to be called men. These sectarians, resorting to mystical Gnostic precepts and abusing the Holy Sacrament of Confession, have taken to misleading a number of their female penitents into believing that the ignominious acts into which they've been initiated are conduits of divine grace and paths to the highest degrees of perfection. This sect is enveloped in a veil of extreme mystery; the sectarian priests pretend to be men of prayer, while the most sanctimonious of their female parishioners are the most assiduous participants in the long, all-too-long, rituals of piety practiced right there in church.

The delivery of these priests into the hands of justice for corruption of minors has shed light on the shameful sect of Palizzolo and revealed to all its secret purpose.

I have only one thing to add to Don Luigi Sturzo's statement. At a certain point he writes that the priests were acting in accordance with "mystical Gnostic precepts." In so doing, Don Luigi to some degree ennobles them. Whereas they haven't acted in accordance with any precepts, or even basic human decency!

The Palizzolo scandal is beginning to resonate across the entire country. A number of high-ranking politicians, such as Turani, Tasca, and others, have even weighed in on the question. We, however, prefer to bring to your attention only the words of a priest of Don Luigi Sturzo's stature, as we believe that such words, coming from such a source, vindicate us against all malicious gossip and base insinuations.

There is, therefore, no conspiracy. Only a love of Truth and Justice.

*

"I was told you're going back to Camporeale this evening, so I've come to say goodbye."

"Thank you, Signor Teresi."

"Captain, if I may: Since I go rather often to Camporeale, I would like to call on you every now and then. Why are you laughing?"

"I just now received a telephone call from my commander. He told me there's a big surprise in store for me, which he'll reveal to me tomorrow, when I return to headquarters. Except that it won't be a surprise to me, since I already know what it is. I'm going to be promoted and transferred."

"*Promoveatur ut amoveatur.*"[5]

"Exactly."

[5] Latin expression meaning: "Have him promoted, to get him out of the way." Nowadays we sometimes say that such a person is "kicked upstairs."

"I'm not sure whether I should congratulate you or be disappointed."

"You can do both. Oh, and listen: I also read that article attacking us and insinuating that we were plotting together . . . "

"Ignoble."

"Exactly. I just hope my uncle doesn't read it, since it was written in a national daily. He's getting on in years, and it would upset him greatly."

"Excuse me for asking, Captain, but who is your—"

"Oh, just a country priest. I lost my father before I was ten. We were poor, and it was this uncle who brought me up and saw me through my studies . . . Everything I have I owe to him, even my character. Well, I'd better be going now, counsel. And be careful . . . I mean it."

"Careful about what?"

"You're Sicilian and you have to ask me, who is from the Piedmont? For now you've won, and they may even hoist you up onto their shoulders . . . "

"You're right, you know. The president of the social club has asked me to resubmit my request for admission. He assured me that the club will be honored to have me as a member. And the mayor has even recommended to the prefect that I be given a knight's cross."

"You see? And yet I'm convinced that, starting tomorrow, you'll be entering the most difficult period of your life. A backlash will come. It's inevitable. I wish you the best of luck."

Chapter XIII
The Wheel Changes Direction

One week later, on the quiet, the bishop of Camporeale sent for Don Mariano Dalli Cardillo. When the aging priest was shown in by Don Marcantonio, His Most Reverend Excellency Egilberto Martire got up from his armchair and greeted him with arms raised to the heavens, as if they were old friends from the seminary.

"Our dear Don Mariano!"

He rested his hands on the other's shoulders, looked him in the eye with one half of his mouth smiling, the other not, then sat him down on the sofa and sat himself down beside him.

"How are things, my dear friend, how are things with you? Not too good, I take it? My own wounds have not yet healed, and I imagine it's the same for you! At any rate, with God's help, we can say we overcame this terribly difficult ordeal the Lord has put before us!"

Don Mariano thought that since His Excellency was speaking to him in Italian, and not Roman dialect, it must mean he was not angry at him.

"And now, to us. I wanted to see you in person, you know, so I could thank you!"

"For what, Your Excellency?"

"For what?! What do you mean, 'for what?' For having demonstrated—by your presence, by your daily practice—that not all the priests of Palizzolo were made of the same matter as those seven base individuals unworthy of their office as shepherds of souls!"

"But, Your Excellency, I—"

"No, no—no modesty, let me tell you outright! You were like the luminous beam of a lighthouse as all the world around you fell into darkness!"

"But, Your Excellency, I did nothing special! I merely kept on doing what I've always done, hearing confessions, comforting the faithful—"

"Giving counsel . . . "

"Also, yes, as needed."

"Well, come to think of it, on the subject of counsel, do you remember the words of our Lord Jesus, when he said: "Give unto Caesar what is Caesar's, and to God what is God's?"

"Of course I remember those words!"

"Have you always kept them foremost in your mind?"

"Yes, sir, I have!"

"Then why is it that when that widow came to you to confess, and asked for your fatherly advice, you consented that she should give to Caesar what should in fact have been given to God?"

Patre Mariano was totally flummoxed.

"But, Your Excellency, I don't know what you're—"

"Let me explain. Unless I am mistaken, when that unfortunate woman, the widow, revealed to you, during confession—during con-fes-sion, mind you—the turpitudes of your confrères, you allowed her, consented, permitted, paved the way for her to go straight to the Royal Carabinieri to report their actions, causing what happened to happen."

"And what should I have done?"

"But, my blessed son, it's priests we're talking about! Ministers of the faith! Anointed by the Lord! Men of God! Priests who had, yes, erred from the straight and narrow path—I'm the first to admit it—but still priests nonetheless! *In aeternum!* You should have given to God what was God's; you should have told that woman to come to me and tell me that a few soldiers of Christ were sullying their cassocks! You forgot,

Don Mariano, that they were wearing frocks, not the uniforms of—I dunno, the royal army or carabinieri! I myself would have taken care of banishing those scoundrels, but with the proper care, and the necessary caution, over time, without creating a scandal . . . Because, let's be frank, the scandal you so carelessly triggered risked shaking the very foundations of the Church!"

"Please forgive me, Your Excellency, I beg you, I implore you to forgive me! But I was so upset by that woman's revelation that I didn't think for a moment that—"

"But I'm not reproaching you in any way! I understand you! I understand you perfectly!"

"To this day, I swear, I still cannot fall asleep. Ever since that woman told me everything, I spend my nights awake, in prayer!"

"Indeed when I saw you come in today, I got scared. I thought you were seriously ill."

"No, Your Excellency, I'm not ill, it's just that this whole business—"

"But you can't carry on like this! With no sleep for a whole week! You're at the end of your rope, my dear friend! You're urgently in need of help! Listen, Don Mariano, shall we do what's best?"

"And what's that?"

"Shall we have you take a nice, long period of rest? Don't say no; you really do need one. Tell you what: in the next two or three days I'll send another priest to relieve you. What do you say?"

"God's will be done."

"Good for you, Don Mariano! Come, let's have a big hug!"

*

"Gentlemen, fellow members, your attention, please. In two days—that is, this next Sunday—at ten o'clock in the morning, all members, as is written on the flyer posted on the showcase window, are invited to vote on the admission to this club of the attorney, Matteo Teresi, who has resubmitted his request," said don Liborio Spartà.

"So we're starting all over with that same bloody headache?" asked Commendatore Paladino.

"But do the rules allow that?" asked Giallonardo in turn.

"The rules allow three admission requests," President Spartà clarified. "And this is Teresi's second request."

"Well, while we're talking about rules," don Anselmo intervened from his damask chair, "I'd like to know whether abstention is allowed, or we must vote only yes or no."

"One who abstains is someone who hasn't the courage of his convictions," declared Colonel Petrosillo.

"And, since you have no convictions whatsoever, you have no need for courage, either," retorted don Anselmo.

"Well, dear sir, for your information, I have been awarded the bronze medal!"

"What was that? I didn't quite hear. What kind of medal?"

"The bronze!"

"Ah, I'm sorry. I thought you'd said the 'pawn's medal.'"

In an effort to wash this terrible slight away with blood, the colonel took off through the air, flying across the salon towards don Anselmo, but was intercepted in midflight by don Stapino Vassallo.

"Consider yourself challenged!" shouted the colonel, foaming at the mouth as he struggled to free himself of don Stapino's embrace.

"Like the last time? When first you challenged me, then you disappeared from circulation?"

"Gentlemen, gentlemen! For goodness' sake!" said the president. "Please calm down. And allow me to clarify something. It was I myself who personally solicited Attorney Teresi's new request."

"Why not just let sleeping dogs lie?" queried don Anselmo.

"Because I consider it the highest of honors for this club to have, as a member, a person who did not hesitate to risk a great deal, to expose himself to personal danger, to—"

"Who's the other sponsor?" Giallonardo interrupted him.

"Our dear mayor."

"I call to your attention that my question has not yet been answered."

"Yes, abstention is allowed."

"Well," said don Anselmo, "I hereby declare that I will abstain."

"Whereas I, this time, will vote 'yes,'" said don Serafino Labianca.

"Did the Grand Lodge order you to do that?" asked Professor Malatesta.

"The Grand Lodge hasn't a bloody thing to do with it! And enough of your priestlike insinuations, you who used to serve Mass with Patre Samonà! And kneel before him to kiss his hand! I'm voting yes because Teresi helped send that renegade Marquis Cammarata to prison!"

"And I'm going to vote 'no,' precisely *because* I used to serve the Mass with Patre Samonà! But don't you realize that this is a plot against the Church?" asked Professor Malatesta.

"Oh, come now! A plot?"

"Gentlemen, gentlemen, this is no time to argue. The voting will take place Sunday morning. We have two more days to think it over. You should each take the time to reflect calmly, and—"

"Mr. President, if I may. Sunday morning is no good," Commendatore Paladino interjected.

"Why not?"

"On my way here I saw some people posting announcements. On Sunday morning there's going to be a great procession of reconciliation, on the orders of the bishop of Camporeale."

"All right, then, we will postpone the meeting until five P.M. that evening. Is everyone in agreement?"

*

"Thank you for inviting me to lunch," said Luigino Chiarapane, whom Stefano had run into by chance that morning in Palizzolo.

"What did you come into town for?" Teresi asked him.

"Well, there's something I didn't really understand, to be honest."

"What do you mean?"

"Three days ago, Zà Ernestina suddenly arrived at our house in Salsetto."

"The marquise?!" Teresi and his nephew said in chorus.

"Yes."

"And what did she want?"

"No idea," said the young man. "At first my mother didn't even want to see her, but Zà Ernestina insisted, and she was crying. So in the end they shut themselves up in Mamma's bedroom and were in there talking for two hours."

"And didn't your mother tell you anything afterwards?" asked Stefano.

"No, nothing. Then, the day before yesterday she came here to Palizzolo."

"To talk to her cousin?"

"Of course. Why else would she come here?"

"Maybe her cousin wants your mother to withdraw her denunciation," said Stefano.

Teresi started laughing.

"Stefanù, I get the feeling that your law school studies . . . Don't you know that at this point nobody can do anything anymore? At most, the marquise could ask the Chiarapane family not to press charges. Which means I would lose a job, since I'm her lawyer. Oh, well . . . "

"But you still haven't told us why you came into town," said Stefano.

"My mother said I had to come to see Zà Ernestina'cause she wants to talk to me. She's expecting me this afternoon at three."

"Just be sure that you don't run into *'u zù* Carmineddru again!" said Stefano.

They all laughed.

"Still, I'm dying of curiosity to know what she wants from you," Stefano added.

"Let's do this. After I go to see her, I'll come back here around five and tell you everything."

But Luigino never returned.

As soon as the procession emerged from the Mother Church, it was clear it was going to be a grand affair.

Preceded by all the municipal police officers in full dress uniform, four priests came out hoisting up a large, gold-embroidered baldachin with His Excellency the bishop of Camporeale sitting inside, holding a monstrance, also gold, in his hand.

Behind him came the four remaining priests of Palizzolo.

And right behind them were Baron Lo Mascolo, Baron Roccamena, Baron Piscopo, and Marquis Spinotta.

Then there was a short space between the nobles and the town council, and in this space was a lone man, all dressed in fustian, shod in boots, and carrying his *coppola* beret in his hand.

After him came Mayor Calandro with the town council and staff, followed by the town businessmen and bourgeois—all of them, from don Liborio and don Anselmo to don Serafino,

Giallonardo the notary, Professor Malatesta, and Colonel Petrosillo . . .

And each—whether noble or bourgeois, businessman or bureaucrat—with his respective wife.

The municipal band separated this group at the head of the procession from the rest of the common folk. Almost three thousand in all, a first.

All the other people who had come out on their balconies and terraces, wearing their Sunday best, knelt down as the procession passed, showering the bishop's baldachin with roses and other flowers.

The procession then headed down the street on which Teresi's house stood. Everyone looked up.

And they saw the lawyer on his balcony with his hat on. Was he trying to taunt them all by keeping his head covered in front of the Most Holy Sacrament? There wasn't a single person in the passing procession who wasn't staring at him. But then, the moment the baldachin was directly under his balcony, Matteo Teresi doffed his hat and made a deep bow.

Not to the Most Holy Sacrament, however, but to the man in fustian walking alone between the nobles and the town council.

And he called to him loudly, shouting above the blare of the band:

"When you see *'u zù* Carmineddru, give him my fondest regards!"

Then he went inside, shutting the doors to the balcony.

"Gentlemen members, I hereby open the voting for the admission of lawyer Matteo Teresi into our club. I remind you that a black marble means 'no,' and a white marble means 'yes.'"

"Please, if I may," said Giallonardo.

"Yes, go ahead."

"Mr. President, when you announced to us the other day

that we would be holding this meeting, something unusual happened. According to the rules, the voting must be secret. Whereas two days ago, two members openly declared what their vote would be. You should have immediately disqualified them. But you didn't. So my question is: are their publicly admitted votes still valid?"

"Please explain what you mean," the president said with some pique.

"I'll cite an example. The last time we met, Professor Malatesta, here present, declared that he would vote against admission. So I now ask the professor, is he still of the same opinion?"

"Of course I'm still of the same opinion! All the more so after what the lawyer did when the procession passed by his house!"

"Speaking of which, who was that man?" asked don Liborio.

"Don't you know?" asked don Serafino. "You're probably the only person here who doesn't. That man is *'u zù* Peppi Timpa, whom we could call *'u zù* Carmineddru's temporary replacement."

"Well, to continue," Giallonardo the notary resumed, "if that's the way it is, then it's clear that the voting will be invalid, since Professor Malatesta's pre-announced black marble will be counted and admission to the club must be based on unanimity. Therefore voting will only be a waste of time."

"So how do we get out of this predicament?"

"I have a suggestion, if I may . . . "

"Please go ahead, sir."

"The novelty of the other day—meaning, the open declaration of a member's vote, which is not explicitly prohibited by the rules and therefore could be admissible—could be of help to us here. You could ask the members how many of them intend to vote no, without them needing to say why."

"Would the gentlemen members who intend to vote no please raise their hands?" asked the president.

Some twenty hands went up. The president turned pale and said not a word. Aside from five or six strict Catholics, all the others must have been people who couldn't bring themselves to accept the public insult made to *'u zù* Peppi Tinca, or whatever the hell his name was.

Giallonardo the notary spoke for the president.

"As you can see, Mr. President, there is no point in voting. My advice is that Signor Teresi, if he's really so keen on it, should submit a third and final request."

The silence that descended upon the salon was broken by don Stapino's cheerful voice.

"Casimiro, bring out the playing cards!"

*

At seven o'clock Monday evening, the town council met to discuss the mayor's proposal to write to the prefect to have Matteo Teresi awarded the title of *cavaliere* and given the knight's cross.

"I would like to speak in a personal capacity," said Mangiameli, a lawyer.

"Please go ahead," said President Burrano.

"I speak as a practicing, observant Catholic. I had been entirely in favor of underwriting the mayor's proposal because I was convinced that my legal colleague Teresi's action against the parish priests who had revoltingly betrayed their divine mission was dictated by a sincere desire for justice. But after what happened yesterday morning during the procession I had to revise my position. He offended the holy solemnity of the occasion! He started shouting in the presence of the Most Holy Sacrament! This I have taken as a clear sign that he hasn't the least bit of respect for our sacred religion!"

"And neither for our sacred Mafia," someone said under his breath, though it was unclear who.

"And therefore," Mangiameli concluded, "I will vote against rewarding Teresi, and nothing can make me change my mind!"

"Permission to speak!" said Pasqualino Marchica, a grain and fava bean merchant.

"Permission granted."

"With all due respect to our mayor, I wouldn't feel right voting yes, either. Matteo Teresi is a man whose opinions I respect, but he's also someone who always comes out guns blazing without thinking twice. He seeks to do the right thing, but without taking into account the harm it might bring to others."

"That's the absolute truth!"

"I'll cite just one example. When he found out what those swinish priests were doing, he took that bucket of shit, and instead of dumping it into the pit, he threw it over the whole town! He covered us all in shit! The priests surely deserved it, but not everyone else. He ruined the lives of four girls who—"

"Five," said another voice.

" . . . five girls who—"

"There are seven of them," suggested another voice.

"Would somebody then please tell me how many goddamn girls there are?" asked Pasqualino Marchica.

"Just one minute," said President Burruano, counting on his fingers. "Paolina Cammarata, Antonietta Lo Mascolo, Totina Perricone, the widow Cannata, Lorenza Spagna, and Filippa Lanza. That makes six."

Pasqualino Marchica resumed speaking.

" . . . ruined the lives of six girls who—"

"Hey, Pasqualì, it doesn't add up!"

"Why not?"

"We're forgetting the dead girl, Rosalia Pampina."

"But she's already dead! Just let me finish! He's ruined the lives of six girls whose only fault was to have believed what their priests told them! These poor young women, whether noble or of humble station, can only become nuns now. They'll never find a husband anymore! Thanks to our fine lawyer friend, all over Italy everyone's talking about Palizzolo as if it was some kind of whorehouse! He's not the kind of man to do the right thing. And so I say no!"

After three hours of discussion, the town council decided to reject the mayor's proposal.

"Montagnet was right," Teresi said to Stefano at the dinner table. "The wheel of fortune is already changing direction. The backlash has begun."

"But you didn't really believe him, since you requested admission to the club a second time. If you had, you wouldn't have made the request, because you would have known that in one way or another they would say no."

"You're right. I didn't believe Montagnet. I thought my fellow townsmen would be a little more grateful. When in fact they're not. No club membership, no knight's cross."

"But did you really care so much?"

"Well, yes and no."

"Zio, you know what your worst fault is? Being an idealist."

"Is that a fault?"

"Well if you don't like the word 'fault,' we can call it a 'shortcoming.'"

"Oh, there's something else I wanted to tell you. I went to the bank today and they told me the manager wanted to talk to me. He never once looked me in the eye; he only said, 'Thank you.' And I said: 'For what?' And he said: 'For having ruined my life, and my family's life. I'm hoping to be transferred out of here as soon as possible.' The poor guy! I really felt sorry for him. But what do I have to do with any of it? I didn't even know that his daughter Filippa was one of the girls involved!

It was the widow Cannata who revealed her name, but the fault is always mine!"

He threw his napkin onto the table and went out onto the balcony.

It was a hot evening. Dark but starry. He pulled a cigar out of his waistcoat pocket and lit a match.

The bullet passed so close to him that it blew out the match.

Chapter XIV
How It All Ended

The following morning was market day.

As he had always done every week, Teresi didn't miss it, despite the fact that the gunshot of the previous evening had cost him a few hours of sleep. You can be as brave as you want, but a bullet whizzing right past your head will never fail to rattle your nerves at least a little. But he did not feel afraid. It was something he'd been expecting, in a sense. *One of these days they're going to shoot me*, he often used to think when some of the more fiery polemics he wrote in his newssheet touched upon untouchable local interests or roiled the already foul waters.

At the market he loved to browse from stall to stall, and especially to chat with the merchants and hawkers, who, in covering the entire province over the course of the week, knew more things than the prefect himself. And since they all knew Teresi well, they would tell him everything: all the stories of infidelity, theft, and fraud, as well as the marriages, births, and deaths that had occurred in the towns they'd just been through. They were better than any local news correspondents could be, of which he had none for his newssheet anyway. Some of these stories actually came in installments, and each week he would get the most recent updates.

That morning, however, as he walked among the people, stopping at each stall, he felt that something around him had changed. Something barely perceptible, but real. A darting glance perhaps, a half smile, a word left hanging . . .

He also noticed another difference. Whereas in the past

he'd always had to shoulder his way through the throng, this time, as soon as people saw him, they stepped aside, almost as if to avoid coming into physical contact with him.

They know! he thought.

The night before, when he went out onto the balcony, he was absolutely certain there wasn't anybody in the street below. And right after the shot, he hadn't heard so much as a window open or close. So how was it that the news of the gunshot had reached the ears of everyone?

"Attorney Teresi!"

He turned around. It was a carabiniere.

"I went to your house looking for you, and your nephew kindly told me I would find you here."

"What is it?"

"Marshal Sciabbarrà wants to see you."

*

"Could you please explain to me why you went directly to the market this morning instead of coming to this station?"

"Why should I have done that?"

"To report what happened last night."

"And what happened?"

"So nothing happened to you last night?"

"Absolutely not," said Teresi with a questioning expression on his face.

"I get it," said the marshal. "So I guess I'm just talking to hear the sound of my own voice."

"If you feel like talking and enjoy doing so, go right ahead."

"No, I don't feel like it, and I don't enjoy doing so. There's nothing enjoyable about it whatsoever. If you find a gunshot that actually blows out the match you just struck to light your cigar enjoyable, that's your business. To each his own. I'm just trying to do my job."

Teresi was flabbergasted. How the hell did the marshal know even the detail about the match? There was no need to ask.

"This town, my good lawyer, is like a sleeping cat. Its eyes are shut, it doesn't move, and we think it's asleep. But in fact the cat is counting the stars in the sky. In this town, nothing ever remains secret. Everyone comes to know everything about everyone. For that reason, I understand perfectly well why you don't feel like reporting the incident. Shall I tell you why?"

"Please."

"First of all, you are correctly convinced that if you did report it, and I began an investigation, it would be like trying to catch the wind. Secondly, any report on your part would, in one way or another, only increase the gossip about you, whereas you, at the present moment, need a little peace and quiet around you."

"You're a very intelligent man, Marshal."

"Thank you. But, to continue, and to keep hearing the sound of my own voice, even if you need a little peace and quiet around you, there's no saying that other people want to grant you this peace and quiet. Eternal peace, perhaps, yes, but a few months of quiet, probably not. Know what I mean?"

"No, I don't really follow."

"My good man, whoever shot at you last night . . . Actually, no, let me rephrase that: Whoever shot at a man lighting his cigar on the balcony last night—"

"—and missed . . . "

"You really think so? Come on, Mr. Teresi, whoever shot at you missed on purpose! He needed only to fire a second time to kill the man on the balcony. But he didn't. He didn't, because his intention was to send you a message. That bullet whizzing past your head was talking to you. And it could only have been saying two things: 'Whatever you've done is done. But from this moment on, be careful what you do.' Is that a little clearer now?"

"Perfectly clear. And what was the second thing?"

"The second thing may have been the following: 'Pack your bags and get out of this town while there's still time.' Clear?"

"Perfectly. And I thank you for your courtesy. Oh, and, listen: Have you got any news of Captain Montagnet?"

"I'm told the good captain left yesterday for his new destination. He's been promoted to major. And he's moving to Alessandria, in the Piedmont. He'll be very happy, I'm sure."

And thus they'd taken away the one friend he could always count on.

*

"Have you heard the news?" asked don Anselmo, entering the club in a rush.

"Yes, we have," don Serafino Labianca, don Stapino Vassallo, and Commendatore Paladino, the only people present, replied almost in unison.

"Attorney Teresi sent his regards to *'u zù* Carmineddru through *'u zù* Peppi Timpa, and *'u zù* Carmineddru didn't waste any time replying," said don Stapino, laughing.

"You think so?" asked don Serafino.

"Why, do you have a better explanation for what happened?"

"I've got more than just one, my friend, as far as that goes. Let's begin by saying it could have been a shrewd move by a father whose daughter has been ruined by the scandal Teresi stirred up. So he shoots at him, unfortunately missing his target, but it's no sweat off his back, because afterwards we're all ready to say that it could only have been *'u zù* Carmineddru or *'u zù* Peppi Timpa that did it."

"It seems to me you're thinking of one person in particular."

"The Marquis Cammarata? No, I would rule him out. But it could have been—just to name one possibility, for the sake of argument—*ragioniere* Toto Lanza."

"The bank manager? No, come on!"

"I'm sorry, but why does that surprise you? Didn't his daughter Filippa end up being the talk of the town because of Teresi? And then Toto Lanza's own history . . . ah, never mind!"

"Oh, no you don't! Now you must tell us everything you know!"

"Just the other day I spoke with the lawyer defending Patre Samonà, who took advantage of Filippa, Lanza's daughter. He said Don Samonà had told him that once, right after he'd finished doing it with the girl, Toto Lanza himself had come into the sacristy. The priest had forgotten to lock the door! Luckily they'd both just put their clothes back on, but Filippa's face was as red as a tomato, one of her tits was hanging halfway out, and it was clear that something had happened between the two. But Toto Lanza said nothing. He just whispered, 'Excuse me,' and went back out."

"But that means he hadn't understood a thing!"

"He'd understood perfectly well, my friend! In fact, one month later he went to Patre Samonà and told him he'd discovered that the priest was a cousin of the bank's president. In short, he asked him to ask his cousin to promote him from teller to manager. And Don Samonà, who realized the man was trying to make a deal with him, did what he needed to do and, one month later, Toto Lanza became the branch manager."

"It's hardly surprising," said don Anselmo. "Toto Lanza actually looks like a cuckold. Cuckolded by his own daughter, and probably also by his wife!"

"That's something you'd have to ask don Cecè Greco, who unfortunately is not present!" said Commendatore Paladino.

It was well-known that Michela Lanza and Cecè Greco had had a thing going for years.

"But there's another possibility," don Serafino resumed. "Which is that nobody at all shot at Teresi."

"What are you saying?! All the neighbors heard the shot!"

"Calm down. I'm saying that Teresi may have told his nephew, Stefano, to go down into the street and fire a shot at him."

"But why would he do that?"

"Because, since nobody saw who fired the shot, Teresi can give the gunman whatever name he wants when he writes about it in his newspaper. And thereby ruin the life of whoever he's got it in for most at that moment. Someone like you, don Stapino, for example. If the man writes that it was you who fired the shot, how will you defend yourself? Sue him for libel? If you sue, then people will start to think it really was you. Take my word for it: there's only one thing we should be hoping for: that next time the gunman doesn't miss."

"But didn't you say you would have voted in favor of admitting him to the club? Have you changed your mind or something?" asked don Anselmo.

"And would you yourself vote to admit a momentarily walking corpse?"

*

"*For pressing family reasons I find myself forced to terminate our association, as I am no longer in need of your services. Regards, Giovanni Galletto.*"

With the above telegram, the fifth of its kind, Matteo Teresi lost the fifth of the six most important cases he was working on. Five telegrams in a single week, almost one a day, all the same, all using the same formula: "*For pressing family reasons . . .* " This was to make him understand, if he hadn't already, that this was all by design, and he would never again be given the kind of case that allowed him to eat, to live his life, to publish his newssheet.

The Mafia, the priests, and the nobles, with these telegrams from his former clients—whom they'd threatened and forced to withdraw their support—were telling him that they intended to reduce him to abject poverty. Because all his other cases—the ones involving the poor, the wretched, the peasants abused by their masters—not only did they not bring him a single lira in revenue, but very often he had to pay for the officially stamped documents and the court fees out of his own pocket.

He had enough money in the bank to live for about two or three months. What would he do afterwards?

"Zio," said Stefano. "I have something to tell you that will upset you, but I have to tell you just the same. You'd even predicted it, actually."

"Go ahead."

"I ran into Luigino."

"So why haven't I heard from him?"

"You'll know in a minute. He told me the Chiarapana family has decided not to press charges."

And there went his sixth and last important case!

"Was that why the marquise went to talk to Luigino's mother?"

"It's not the only reason."

"There's more?"

"Yes. The scheme's a little more complicated . . . "

"Go on, don't be shy."

"Luigino's gonna go to the carabinieri and tell them it was him who got Paolina pregnant, letting Patre Terranova off the hook. Terranova will swear he never laid a hand on Paolina, and only abused the widow and Totina—both legal adults—on the day at the convent. That way he gets out of the more serious charge of corrupting a minor, and the marquis gets to claim the usual extenuating circumstance of defending family honor for the crime of attempted murder of Luigino, which on top of everything else he failed to complete."

Attorney Teresi had become so pale that Stefano got scared he might be having a heart attack.

"Drink a little water, Zio."

"So what does Luigino get out of this?"

"He gets married to Paolina and they make him a rich man. They pay off all his father's debts, which are considerable, he gets the Cammaratas' palazzo in Salsetto, as is, and they're going to give him their Zummìa estate in the dowry."

"So, I guess it all works out."

"And you want to know something else?"

"Tell me."

"I ran into Baron Lo Mascolo by chance. He said he wants to talk to me."

*

Three mornings later, the postman delivered a stamped envelope from the Criminal Court of Camporeale. Teresi opened it. There was a letter dated September 10 and signed by the presiding judge, Gianfilippo Smecca, a man always ready to adjust his sails to catch the prevailing winds.

Illustrious sir,

This communication is to inform you that your presence is required on the 15th day of the current month, at 17:00 hours at the Court of Camporeale, via Regina Margherita 10, for a hearing with the Disciplinary Committee pursuant to the charge of professionally inappropriate behavior, as raised against your person by all of the criminal lawyers practicing in the City of Palizzolo.

The charge stems from the fact that, on the occasion of the well-known case that led to the arrest of Marquis Filadelfo Cammarata, you accumulated unto yourself a series of positions that lead one to conclude the existence of a pre-existing, personal hostility, on your part, towards the abovementioned Marquis.

They are, in order:

Plaintiff (presenting yourself as such to the Royal Carabinieri);

Witness for the prosecution (presenting yourself as such to the Investigating Magistrate);

Attorney for Plaintiff (as designated by the Chiarapane family, a role accepted by you though later revoked by the same family).

It behooves us to inform you, moreover, that Signora Albasia Chiarapane sent us, of her own accord a declaration in which she asserts that, to the end of filing together, as one, a denunciation with the Royal Carabinieri, you demanded of her a sum of ten thousand lire in cash, claiming that you would otherwise "wash your hands of the whole affair."

We must also remind you that the Disciplinary Committee has the right to proceed even in the absence of the person under disciplinary investigation.

Regards,

Naturally, Matteo Teresi had no desire to appear at the hearing. And even if he did appear, what could he possibly say in his defense? The most serious charge was not that of having played three roles in a farce—which was actually true—but of having taken ten thousand lire to go and report the attempted murder of Luigino. The accusation was patently false, but how would he ever prove it? By this point it was clear that they were all in agreement to get him out of their hair, in one way or another. But he still had his newssheet, and as long as he still had the money to publish it, no one would ever succeed in silencing him.

*

In the evening after receiving the letter from the Criminal Court, he didn't feel like eating.

Clearly, it would turn out one of two ways: either they would impose a long period of suspension on him, or they would strike him from the lists. The second was the more likely.

He would have to abandon the paupers who turned to him for help, leave them to their fate as the wretched of the earth.

Not that he'd won so many of his cases on behalf of the poor; the law always came down on the side of the rich. But at least they'd served to give a little hope to those who'd never known any hope at all.

He felt empty inside, however, and a little confused. The fact was that he was used to fighting out in the open, to going hand-to-hand, even to being insulted, but not to treacherous surprise attacks, stabs in the back in the dark and in secret. They were scorching the earth all around him, and to set it on fire they were using the hands of those who had nothing in particular against him but couldn't or didn't know how to say no to those who asked them to light the match.

He went to bed early, read a bit of *Don Quixote*, which he always kept on his bedside table, then slowly, little by little, fell asleep with the light on.

The sound of the front door opening and closing woke him up. He looked at his watch: it was past midnight.

Where had Stefano been all this time?

"Stefano."

"I'll be right there, Zio."

Seeing the young man come in, he knew at once from the look on his face that he had news.

"I've been with Baron Lo Mascolo. He invited me to dinner."

"With the whole family?"

"No, just me and him."

"What did he want?"

Stefano sat down on the edge of the bed.

"That baron's got a real poker face, but in the end he tells you exactly what's on his mind."

"And what's on his mind?"

"Zio, it took him at least three hours to explain the whole business to me. He made the most convoluted arguments, going round and round in concentric circles, all the while zeroing in on the point he wanted to make."

"And what was that?"

"The point was sort of a copy of what the Marquis Cammarata did."

"Explain."

"What's to explain, Zio? Can't you figure it out for yourself?" said Stefano, a little irritated.

"I get it, Stefanù. Antonietta will testify that Patre Raccuglia wasn't the first man in her life. It was you who got her pregnant. Right?"

"Right."

"So Patre Raccuglia wriggles out of the charge of corrupting a minor, just like Patre Terranova. And you take Antonietta, an only child, for your wife, and you get rich. Right?"

"Right."

"And did you start slapping him?"

"No."

"Did you laugh in his face?"

"Not even."

"But, Stefanù, this stuff is straight out of the puppet theatre! Do you realize that?"

Stefano stood up.

"Yes, I do, but there's something you don't realize."

"And what's that?"

"That I actually love Antonietta. But I told the baron I couldn't accept. Out of respect for you, Zio."

*

The following morning the postman handed him a letter from America.

Teresi recognized the handwriting. It was his brother Agostino writing to him.

Two years older than Matteo, Agostino had married an American cousin of his, moved to New York, and made a fortune buying and selling homes. He had three children, all girls. The oldest, Carmela, had married an engineer who worked for her father, and had two children. Agostino and Matteo customarily wrote to each other once a month.

In the present letter, after giving the usual news about his wife, daughters and grandchildren, Agostino wrote:

And so, dear brother, chatting the other day with my wife, she asked me a question I had no answer for. She said: "But what's your brother Matteo doing still hanging around Palizzolo? Since the death of your parents, he's more alone than a dog. If he came here to live, he would be among family again." I didn't know what to say. But I did think that you might have answered the question with a question: "And what on earth would I do in New York?" Dear Matteo, there's a great deal of things that someone like you could do here. There are so many wretchedly poor immigrants who are treated worse than our peasants in Palizzolo! You have no idea the kinds of conditions they're forced to live in! And there's something else, too. I have a great business opportunity within my reach. There's this big pharmacy, and . . .

Right, because Matteo had first taken a pharmaceutical degree before studying law. He'd almost forgotten.

*

The real blow, however, the kind that lays you flat out on the ground to the point where you can't get back up, came in the form of seven lines signed by His Excellency the Prefect of Camporeale.

We inform you that we have ratified the request of the Commissioner of Police to revoke your authorization to publish the weekly newssheet entitled The Battle, *printed by Mazzullo & Sons Printworks, granted by the Court of Camporeale on February 12, 1897, and addressed to you, Matteo Teresi, as editor in chief and publisher. This revocation, effective immediately and for an indeterminate amount of time, is dictated by the fact that you have been distributing seditious tracts and passing them off as special editions of your weekly, without, moreover, the proper authorization for such editions.*

And so, for the first time since the wheel of fortune had changed direction, Matteo Teresi felt his face wet with tears.

*

He spent the whole day dawdling about the house. In shirtsleeves, hair disheveled, slippers on his feet, he wandered from room to room, adjusting a book on a shelf or a lamp on a table, straightening a picture on the wall, dusting off some old photos on the living-room bookcase. At half past noon he mechanically set the table for Stefano and himself—even though he knew that nothing had been cooked because it was the housekeeper's day off, and he hadn't even lit the wood in the stove. So he just sat there staring at the empty plates.

But where was Stefano? Why hadn't he come home? Then

Teresi remembered that his nephew had told him the night before that he was leaving for Palermo early that morning to take an exam and would be away for three days. The fact had entirely slipped from his mind. He went upstairs and into the young man's bedroom. The bed was unmade, the wardrobe was missing a suit, and the suitcase was gone. Yes, he'd gone away to take his exam.

Then Teresi went into his own bedroom. Feeling a little feverish, he took the thermometer from the nightstand drawer, lay down, and took his temperature. 99.9. He didn't feel sick, however. It was only the effect of the terrible blow.

He felt a great weight on his eyes, and closed them.

When he awoke, the sun was setting. So he got up and went out on the balcony. He needed some fresh air.

Just some thirty yards past his house, the street he lived on began to descend towards the countryside, and so, at that hour, it was always busy with peasants who had come into town to sell fruits and vegetables and were now on their way home.

He knew them all, every single one of them, and every evening was a rich exchange of greetings. That evening, however, nobody looked up towards his balcony; it was as if he hadn't come out.

"Gnaziu!" he called.

Gnaziu Pirrera was one of the poor devils he had helped out. A father of five, he managed to eat about every other day, and every so often Teresi would give him a little money to feed his children.

Gnaziu Pirrera seemed not to have heard, and kept on walking, eyes on the ground.

*

Night fell ever so slowly.

And when it was completely dark he went back into his

bedroom, grabbed the cigar box and a small box of matches, went back out on the balcony, and lit the first cigar, keeping the match burning as long as possible in front of his face.

If he was waiting, hoping, for the gunshot that this time would blow out not the match but his own life, he was disappointed. Nothing happened.

The night was still. It breathed slowly and restfully, as a scent of straw scorched all day by the sun rose up from the countryside.

*

By one o'clock in the morning, he got tired of staying up. How long had it been since he'd eaten, anyway? He went into the bedroom, grabbed a chair, took it outside, and sat down. He wasn't thinking about the letter from the Prefect, nor about the one from the Criminal Court.

Only Stefano's words were pounding in his head.

"You don't realize that I actually love Antonietta."

And also:

"I told the baron I couldn't accept. Out of respect for you, Zio."

So, Stefano needed to lose the respect he felt for him. If he disappeared from Stefano's life without a word of explanation, maybe the lad would feel betrayed. And that would free him to choose his own destiny. Yes. That was the only solution.

Little by little, the idea gained strength. When the sky began to lighten in the east, the idea became a firm decision.

He looked at his watch. Five o'clock in the morning.

So, if he immediately started packing his bags, then bathed and shaved and put on a nice suit, he could easily catch the coach to Palermo after dropping in at the bank and withdrawing all his money. It would be more than enough to buy a ticket to America on the first ship out.

Author's Note

This novel purposely distorts real events that took place in a Sicilian town, Alia, at the start of the twentieth century, to the point of rendering them so unrecognizable as to border on sheer fantasy. A priest by the name of Rosolino Martino was arrested for corruption of underage girls. A former local pharmacist turned lawyer, Matteo Teresi—who in the pages of his weekly newspaper, *La Battaglia*, fought the abuses of mafiosi, landowners, and the clergy—began an investigation of the case and came to the shocking discovery that the priests of Alia had founded a secret sect that "brought together inexperienced, virgin young girls and young brides, deceiving them into believing that sexual relations, and the sexual practices preparatory to the sex act, were a means for acquiring divine indulgences and opening the gates of Heaven," as explained by Gaetano D'Andrea, ex-mayor of Alia.

The discovery of the sect and its practices, when publicized by Teresi, sent shock waves beyond the island of Sicily and elicited the indignation of many political and religious officials, including Filippo Turati and Don Luigi Sturzo. The priest Rosolino Martino confirmed what Teresi had written in his newsweekly.

The clergy, the landowners, and the Mafia, however, closed ranks. On the one hand they attacked Teresi, on the other they forced the population—even the immediate families of the victims of the abuse—to remain absolutely silent on the matter.

Dismayed by the lack of reaction on the part of his fellow townspeople, Teresi goaded them harshly:

"The men are now resigned to the religious prostitution of their women, since it is no longer admissible [. . .], after what has happened, to plead ignorance. Let us avoid this danger, let us open the eyes of husbands and fathers, and after we speak to them frankly and boldly, things will reacquire their proper names. *Divine grace* will no longer be a cover for sexual relations; the mystical bride will seem a common prostitute; the husband, amidst the saints with their haloes, will see his horns sprout majestically twisted; the young woman already on the path to perfection, setting aside her saintly mask, if not yet the mother of some scion of angels will be like the half-virgin of the French, who has lost everything and given everything except her supposed honor, which resides in the simple physiological sign of her virginity."

The article, which appeared in the August 11, 1901, edition of *La Battaglia*, achieved the opposite result, eliciting a wave of genuine hatred towards its author. The bishop of Cefalù accused him of blasphemy and held a reparative procession onto which Teresi, from his balcony, dropped flyers further denouncing the misdeeds of the clergy.

It amounted to underwriting a death sentence for himself. After a warning, Teresi wrote a last article of goodbye in his newsweekly, and took ship for the United States.

In the town of Rochester, New York, he continued practicing his profession as a lawyer and wrote a tremendous number of articles in support of the Italian immigrant community and on such broad questions as divorce and abortion.

His "American" writings were published in 1925, by D'Antoni Editori, a Palermo publishing house, under the title

Con la patria nel cuore ("With the Homeland in My Heart"). They were republished in an anastatic printing, edited by the Comune di Alia, in 2001, with a preface by Gaetano D'Andrea.

To repeat: the reader should consider this novel a product of my own imagination. Only two things were drawn from reality: the names of the protagonist and his newssheet (I did this in homage), and the passage from the article by Don Luigi Sturzo.

Should any reader encounter names or situations reminiscent of real-life names or situations, they should be attributed to chance.

I dedicate this book to Rosetta, for the more than fifty years of life we have spent together.

A.C.

About the Author

Andrea Camilleri is widely considered to be one of Italy's greatest living writers. His Montalbano crime series, each installment of which is a bestseller in Italy, is published in America by Penguin Random House, and several books in the series have been *New York Times* bestsellers.